WEEP, WOMAN, WEEP

MARIA DEBLASSIE

KITCHEN WITCH PRESS

Published by Kitchen Witch Press

NOTE

Typos are the bane of any writer's existence. Like weeds, they pop up every time you think you're done with them. If you should find a typo in the story, email me at mdeblassie@gmail.com and I will give you a free copy of one of my other publications.

WEEP, WOMAN, WEEP

I am built for tears.

It's in my blood. The women in my family didn't know how to have a life without sorrows. If they couldn't find any, they made them.

I was always finding ways to punish myself if I got too happy. I'd get excited about the paperbacks—bodice rippers, mostly—that I'd buy from the used bookstore on the corner of Main Street, and if I liked the ending of one too much, I'd throw it out. Couldn't do with too much happiness in the house.

We were not allowed the things that made us want to rise up like sunflowers. Our mothers weren't allowed them, so we couldn't have them either. My mom used to hide her secret chocolate stash in one of the rusty tin cans she collected, always half-cutting herself when she reached in for something sweet. It was like she couldn't taste the melty goodness without reminding herself that the world was full of sharp, ugly things. Suppose that's where I got it from.

When I look back on things, I always remember the way she seemed to shrink with age. She had the thin bones and pale face of the Spanish—something I hadn't inherited with my tall frame and tan skin. She always looked frailer than she was somehow, like the years working at the local diner slowly ate away at her.

She didn't used to be that way.

I have this memory of her from when I was very young. She looked so fresh and happy, hanging the laundry up on the line, the wind whipping through her hair and kicking up her skirt as she sang her cantos. I mean, she was all sunshine and freshly washed sheets. She had this knack, too, for growing things. Like she could just reach down and touch the earth and know what it needed. That was before I knew about all the bruises and heartache hidden under a buttoned-up dress. Before he left her with a pile of bills and loneliness and me.

I didn't know my father, but I didn't like what he left behind, so I was glad I never had to look at him. All I knew was one day she had me, inherited a small adobe house on a couple acres of land next to the Bosque—we were all that was left of our family—and spent the rest of her life trying to keep that roof over our heads and men from the house.

I used to stay awake at night, trying to figure out ways not to turn out like that.

Wait. Let me back up a bit, so you know where all this was taking place.

We lived in a semi-rural small town in the middle of nowhere called Sueño.

It was more like a bunch of farms and adobe homes sitting on feral acreage with a main street that held everything together. That street was framed by a few blocks of housing that tried to look like a suburb but failed miserably. So, it was a main street, fake suburbs, and farmland contained by the Bosque, with the Rio Grande cutting through it on one side and open desert that seemed to go on forever on the other. My favorite part of all this was the mountains just behind the Rio Grande that turned pink and red like a schoolgirl thinking dirty thoughts when the sun rose and set each day.

People were always forgetting about the town of Sueño. Course, that probably had something to do with the fact that we were located so close to the Shadow Lands—that long sweep of desert between towns and Native lands that just sort of folded in on itself and went on forever. Its own place outside the laws of time and space. Sometimes, people went out there and never came back. Sometimes they did, and you wished they hadn't. Sometimes women went to the outskirts for help, looking for La Huesera, the Bone Woman, to deal with their man troubles. For a price. Least, that's what the old folks said when they were getting ready to spin some impossible yarn and wanted to scare us good.

Me? I didn't bother myself with the Shadow Lands too much because I had my hands full with this whole La Llorona situation and wasn't looking to borrow trouble. La Llorona—she's the Weeping Woman, but I'll get to that in a bit.

The closest city to us was Esperanza, which most people also forgot about unless you lived around these parts. I mean, more than they forgot that New Mexico was part of the United States, which happens more than you think, even now. Esperanza is about an hour away from Albuquerque, the biggest city in New Mexico, and about two hours south of Santa Fe, the capital, where rich white people go to find themselves and feel "cultural." That's the rub with growing up here: We were taught to be ashamed of our heritage, and here are white people dying to be the great-granddaughter of an Indian princess and the long-lost child of a bruja.

I went to Santa Fe once for a field trip, and the most I can remember was that it seemed to have more crosses and churches than Sueño, and that was saying something! And so many white people, I actually felt brown without trying to darken my skin in the sun or pretend to know Spanish. Whereas in Sueño, I could almost pass for white, not that I wanted to. I'd also gone to Albuquerque a time or two, but that city always felt too big for me. Esperanza, on the other hand, felt just big enough to get lost in, but small enough to feel like you wouldn't get swallowed up. Me and Sherry always thought of it as The Big City, but really it was like a big small town.

Esperanza was where you went when you wanted to be forgotten by the place you came from. That was the place you went to reinvent yourself. That was the place me and Sherry had fixed on to escape this hellhole soon as we could.

◆

There, I went and got ahead of myself again and forgot that you don't know about Sherry yet.

Sometimes it still hurts to think of her. But when I do, I like to recall who she was before we were taken. You might think we looked the same because we both had long black hair, and brown eyes, and skin that wasn't quite white. But that's where the similarities ended. I had freckled skin and was more knees and elbows than anything, with sharp features that were more striking than beautiful.

Sherry, on the other hand, was always kind of...luscious. That's the only word for it. She was soft all over with a round face, wide eyes, and a big, full mouth. When puberty hit, she had curves in all the right places while I patiently waited for my chest to fill in more and tried not to be disappointed when it didn't. Even her name was luscious. Sherry—that was back when people favored white names, as if it would erase our bronze skin or at least make it lighter. Now? Everyone's giving their babies Indian, and Mexican, and Spanish, and mixed names, like there was never a time when we were taught to feel shame for those impure bloodlines. Me? I still remember when we were told not to spend too much time out in the sun. Didn't want our skin any darker than it already was. And nobody spoke Spanish to us because they didn't want to dirty our tongues.

Course, my mom was the radical and kept singing in Spanish even though she refused to pass the language on to me.

Anyway, me and Sherry spent most of our days avoiding La Llorona. Yeah, that was her name, the Weeping Woman, like I said before. Maybe you've heard of her? The Rio Grande was our stomping ground. We figured it was best to know everything about La Llorona's natural habitat, all the better to avoid her. Plus, Main Street was full of people we'd rather not see. When we got tired of the river, we walked up and down the acequias and ditches, which could sometimes look like rivers when they were fat and full of rain. But those were dangerous, too, since La Llorona used any watery highway to do her business. And when we got too scared of hanging around water all the time, especially after triple-dog-daring each other to stick our hands in the water and telling her to come get us, we re-treated into the Bosque, where the cottonwoods shielded us from her gaze.

Sherry spent more time at my house or along the river because her mother was a terrible drunk, and the men she allowed in were even worse. But when she had to, she went home to a rundown adobe on a trashed half-acre, right before things started looking more like a formal neighborhood. Neither of us had any siblings, so we pretended we were sisters from different misters. In all honesty, we could have been sisters from the same mister. Sherry didn't know who her dad was either, and the men in this town liked to get around.

Of course, that made us easy pickings for the Weeping Woman.

She liked us pale, silent, and ashamed of our-selves because of things we had no control over. We'd already lasted longer than most girls. That was because we stayed loud and unruly and didn't worry about the sun darkening our skin or what people said about us or our mamas. We were brave in the daylight and didn't let anyone or anything hold us down.

But when the sun sank and darkness fell, our fearlessness went with it. We knew the river woman was coming for us. It was only a matter of time.

♦

So, the way the story goes—the one that gets told in schools and on chilly autumn nights—is that once there was this señorita, and she was the most beautiful woman in the town, and she knew it, too. So, she wouldn't settle for anything less than a rich vaquero. One day, a cowboy just like that rode into town, and she strung him along until he was so dizzy with wanting, he married her. She enjoyed the power she had over him and loved being the hard-won prize.

And enjoy her he did—to the fullest—until she grew round with child, and he lost interest. That's how it happens sometimes, once you have something. Anyway, she had children, and he stopped coming to her at night after the second child. Eventually, she found out that he was cheating on her.

By then, many years had passed, and she was no longer the fiery beauty she once was, and all he did was laugh and laugh at her outrage. You see, he was a little mean-spirited, too, just like her, and enjoyed seeing her suffer in the way she made him suffer all those years ago during their courtship.

Well, when she figured out that was how he really felt about her, she flew into a rage and took their children down to the Rio Grande and drowned them. If she couldn't have the love of that handsome vaquero—he was a prize, too—no one could, not even their kids.

According to legend, once she'd done that, she realized her horrible mistake and tried to get her children back, but by then, it was too late. She roamed the riverbank, wailing for her lost children, and cried so long and hard that her tears got swept up in the river that drowned her, too.

To this day, she still roams that riverbank, looking for her children. You can hear her on stormy nights, weeping and wailing for all she lost. And if you're unlucky enough to catch her eye, she'll take you down into her watery grave, thinking you're one of her kids.

Every time I hear her cries, a shudder goes through me because I know she's looking for me.

♦

Of course, that's the story they tell, and most of it's true.

Here's the part they don't tell you. The thing I'm more and more sure about with each passing year: She didn't regret drowning her kids. She regretted giving up her power to that man. And she regretted being bested by him. He was supposed to help her purify the family line, cleanse her family of tainted blood from unholy mixed unions. They would be reborn through children paler than themselves. Instead, all he brought her was more shame.

The other part most people overlook is that those children were actually girls, and he stopped going to her at night because she couldn't produce a son, the only kind of child that mattered. Back then, you weren't really a woman if you couldn't bear a male heir. So, she was no longer useful to him, and he discarded her, and she was left with nothing but the memory of the power she once had over the man who now pitied and despised her.

La Llorona drowned her girls, not just to spite her husband but to rid herself of two things that would grow up to be more beautiful than her and break her heart all over again when it was time for them to get married. Sherry thought she was protecting them from her fate. I thought her bitter spirit didn't want her daughters doing better than she did. Who knew which version was right?

All I knew was that it wasn't safe to walk alone at night along the riverbank.

♦

Sherry—now she had a good name. Luscious, like I said earlier. Like "Sherry, Baby" the song, like the kind of woman who knows how to have a good time.

Me? I hated my name. Mercy. It sounded like the start of one of those boring sermons we had to suffer through on Sundays. Like the prim and proper pale girls we hated so much. The ones with their long, wet hair pulled back in severe buns and skin the color of bloated fish gone belly-up in the river. Which was what they were once she got them.

Mercy. Sherry knew I hated that name, so she used it when she was irritated with me or just looking to blow off steam after one of her momma's boyfriends blew off steam on her. Sherry could make it sound like a curse or a Hail Mary, and honestly, I didn't know which was worse.

When we fought—we were hot-tempered girls, and I'm not going to pretend we didn't—Sherry knew just how to push my buttons. She'd pester and tease and tell me I had a name that would make me perfect for La Llorona's little collection, chasing me up and down the riverbank with her sharp-tongued taunts. Those would be the times I'd finally give up talking sense to her and hide in a grove of Russian olive trees where the riverbank kissed the Bosque. Their silvery leaves would hug me close to soften the sting of Sherry's words, reminding me that I didn't have to be a Mercy if I didn't want to. I loved her, sure, but she had a mean streak, just like the next person.

But when things were good, usually when one of her "uncles" blew town, or she was feeling fine and powerful after filching some makeup at the drug store, she let me be a Margarita or a Josefina or anyone but Mercy. I changed my mind about them week to week, mostly because I fell in love with any name that was long and smooth on the tongue like a passionate love affair.

I would never be as cool as Sherry, but that didn't stop me from dreaming.

◆

People said she drowned her victims, but I knew the truth of it. It wasn't a drowning.

It was a baptism.

Then you became like the women we always made fun of: Jesus-loving, self-righteous prigs who called themselves Spanish—the closest thing to white they could be—when anyone could see they had the flat nose and dark skin of people who had been here longer than those colonizers.

You could always tell which ones they were, too. Even with their hair up, there was always a wet ring around their tight lace collars. Their eyes were forever red-rimmed, like they'd been crying, though they never did. That's because their hearts stopped once they were baptized, and feelings were things they left at the bottom of the river along with their souls.

Those were the women who married men who cheated and raised mama's boys and little girls so full of their own virtue, they were hard and sour like lemons. Those were the women who cried when their husbands beat them and strayed, then defended them to anyone who said "boo." Love was just a word in country songs, not something you actually got in life.

That's men, and you were lucky if you got one who could be a good provider and sometimes drink so much they forgot to take their pain out on you. Passion, genuine affection, a relationship of equals—those were things that only existed in between the pages of the cheap books me and Sherry guiltily consumed, then cast aside like used condoms.

But I wanted it to be real. So did Sherry.

That's why we promised each other that we would never be like them. It was a vow we renewed every day along the river, like if we said it often enough, we could make it true.

♦

I lied earlier when I said I never knew my father. It's more like I don't remember much about him. Well, that's not entirely true either. I just don't like to think about him. He always had a short fuse, but I never saw him do anything—nothing physical, I mean. It was always the suggestion of it. The arguing when they thought I was asleep. My mom sending me outside to play when things felt testy. I'd go out to our few acres of land until the yelling died down, trying to look invisible.

When things got really loud, I sometimes would sneak over the coyote fence between our home and Mr. Consuelo's farm and hide behind one of his cottonwood trees until the sun set and the yelling stopped. The fence was close to Mr. Consuelo's house, and I often marveled at how he never found me there, hiding behind that lone tree.

You might wonder at a small kid out alone at night, but I wasn't afraid. At least, not about what was outside. I was too young to know about La Llorona, and anyway, I wasn't by the river. The thing was, there was something to the sound of crickets and cicadas at night—a soothing drone that filled my head as I huddled under that tree. It was enough to tune out the violence coming from my adobe. The weeds and wildflowers on our land would crane their faces toward me as I walked past, letting me know I was not alone, and the cotton-wood shielded me from any adults looking to take me from my hiding spot. In the mornings, there would be no evidence of the fighting except the bruises along my mom's forearms when she rolled up her sleeves to make tortillas.

I was pretty young when he left—five? Maybe six? Memories are muddy at that age, but I do remember one thing clearly: I was glad he left, even if he did ruin my birthday from then on. I remember begging my mom for a fancy birthday cake like I saw in the grocery store bakery displays, with pink icing piped into the shape of roses. For weeks, I begged, and she actually made one for me but mixed up the sugar with salt so that it was this sharp, sour mess.

The thing about that cake was that it looked beautiful but tasted disgusting, and I said so—there was no point in lying. We'd all had a mouthful and knew the truth of it. I was just young enough not to know anything about social niceties.

So, my father, he'd been drinking and hated the whole idea of having to be home celebrating a birthday for a kid who was too young to remember it when he could be out playing poker with friends, and he just lost it. I mean really lost it. He forced me to eat that cake, even though it was terrible, and I started crying, and he told me not to cry, but I couldn't stop. Couldn't keep the cake down either. Finally, he grabbed a fistful of my hair and a fistful of the cake and shoved it in my mouth so hard, I started choking. The last thing I remember was my mom was screaming and the taste of salt in my mouth, and then it all went dark.

When I came to, I was tucked in bed, cleaned up, and in my favorite pajamas. My mother sat beside me, running her soft hands over my forehead. When I opened my eyes, she told me that my dad had gone and wasn't ever coming back. That I was safe. Her fingernails were caked in dirt, and her hair looked plastered in sweat. Her dress, too, was wrinkly and damp, like it looked when she'd been mopping the floors. But her face was so strangely calm that I almost believed her.

That next morning, I saw that the kitchen was completely clean, all evidence of my birthday, down to that awful cake, gone. She made me fresh tortillas and scrambled eggs for breakfast and said things would be better from here on out. But that didn't mean anything to me at the time.

He usually left for a few days after a blowout, then came back with cheap gifts and promises to do better. It was a few weeks before I realized that he really wasn't coming back. My mother seemed to know the truth of it, though, that things were never going to be the same.

And they weren't. She got a job at the local diner and made enough with that and a few odd jobs here and there to keep a roof over our heads. Then, once the town was convinced her husband had left her for good, she refused to entertain the attentions of any interested men in town. She also stopped growing things around then. Like she couldn't get things to live properly. Like she wanted to but just couldn't.

After that, my mom always made a big deal about making whatever cake I wanted for my birthday, and if we didn't like it, we never had to finish it. And if we did, she'd make a second one just because. I don't remember all of my birthdays, but I do remember that one, despite him thinking I wouldn't.

There, I went and ruined cake for you. Birthdays, too. See why I don't like to think about my dad?

♦

This is the kind of thing that gets passed down. Either La Llorona takes you, or you are born with her mark because some woman in your family tree got baptized down the line and passed that mark on to all the women who came after her. Eventually, the blood begins to thin that bond so much that we almost seem like regular women.

My mother, for example, was third-generation baptized, which is why she was full of sorrows but didn't show it like the women with the wet hair and bloodshot eyes. She was never formally taken, you see. She just took on the sorrows of her mother and grandmother before her. It was impossible not to. Sad stories were written in our blood. I was fourth generation, which meant La Llorona had her eye on me. Her hold on me was weaker, only a faint trace in my blood, so I knew she would make a point of bringing us—me and the women who came after me—back into the fold.

Sherry was fourth generation, too. But here's the difference between my mom and Sherry's: My mom told me, once I was old enough, that I never had to do anything with any man that I didn't want to. I didn't even have to get married at all if I didn't like the idea. I had options—probably ones we'd never thought up yet—and I got to choose what I wanted to do with my life. That was the first and only time we ever talked directly about my dad, but I knew what she was telling me. She wouldn't hold me back.

Now that was a big deal, in case you didn't realize that yet.

That's because once La Llorona gets one of the women in your family, it's a hard thing to shake. Take Sherry and her mom. Her momma fed the sorrow rather than fight it like my momma and made it harder for Sherry, though she tried not to let it get to her any more than she'd let the unmarked girls fill her with envy.

You know the girls I'm talking about. The ones that didn't have baptisms in their blood and whose mothers loved them enough not to let them stray along the river when the sun set and the shadows grew long. They got an education and moved away, and sometimes they came back, but they didn't live the kind of lives we did. They got the nicer houses and the nicer husbands.

Sometimes they were stupid, though.

They didn't know the kind of freedom they had, so they flirted with things they didn't understand and the next day woke up on the riverbank marked and craving Jesus something fierce. Those girls? They did that to themselves, and though I pitied them for their stupidity, I also hated them for throwing something as precious as their freedom away on a childish rebellion.

As for me, I never stood a chance. I was always marked. La Llorona got the women in my family—always had—and so I knew I was next, even though I fought it tooth and nail.

◆

I liked school okay back then but spent more time figuring out how to make money. Concrete numbers and plans I could hold on to always mattered more to me than making math problems out of triangles. I had enough problems of my own and didn't need more from a class that made a square sound more complicated than it was.

Most days, I was up early, working at Mr. Consuelo's farm across the way before school, then after school, I went to another farm up the road. I loved being up before the sun, with the mountains in the distance and the shimmering cottonwoods of the Bosque like guardian angels watching over me as I went about my day. They were things that soothed me when my fear of being baptized got to be too much.

I was good with plants, too, and anything that came from the land, really. My mom had the same knack and used to make things grow from nothing but dirt and a chipped pot. But she never did anything with the land she'd inherited from her mother, just kept collecting seeds and sometimes planted them in the pots on our porch. Then after my dad left, well, it was like she'd touch things, really get things started, and then let them wither and die before they had a chance to even get established.

I'd come home to the crumpled bodies of dried-out sprouts spread across cracked dirt in little clay pots. I sometimes wondered how she dealt with the sadness of those dead seeds, but then I figured she probably couldn't feel them as strongly as I did. Or maybe double shifts at the diner sucked away her ability to care. Either way, she was great at getting things started. Finishing? Not so much. Me, on the other hand? It was like I could talk to things and listen to what they needed, and they loved me for it. Sherry thought I was crazy for thinking like that, but she'd never understood how beautiful a handful of seeds could be, or what it was like to be comforted by Russian olive trees when she was going through one of her violent spells.

On the weekends, I picked up odd jobs painting barns, building fences, pulling weeds, mucking out stables. Anything to earn a buck and keep my mind off La Llorona. There was always work to do at one of the neighboring farms or nearby houses. I'd thought of working at the store or one of the two restaurants in town (really a diner and a bar), but I didn't like people much and didn't have the soft easiness of Sherry.

My mom got Sherry a job at the diner once she was old enough, though, and she seemed to do okay. Still, working outdoors suited me better, and the farmers weren't shy about paying in cash for odd jobs. I liked the way the wadded bills felt in my fist after a day of hard work. Plus, this work wasn't exactly ladylike, so I figured that was extra insurance against La Llorona, who liked us frail as church mice in Sunday dresses.

So, I'd been working since I was old enough to hustle up some business. I'd been saving since Mr. Consuelo—he owned the big farm next to me and my mom, like I said—gave me my first job, harvesting chicken eggs when I was about twelve or so. He had hair graying around the temples and skin darkened by the sun and a gently wrinkled face that somehow made him more distinguished rather than just old.

He wasn't lean, precisely, but he wasn't sporting a beer belly either. He was just solid, like the earth. All hard labor and a kind heart. Come to think of it, Mr. Consuelo was the only kind man I knew at the time, and even then, I was skittish because I'd heard so many awful stories about what men got up to behind closed doors. That and I never did learn anything about his wife's mysterious passing which happened years before I started working for him.

Me and Sherry used to think up dreadful stories about how he murdered her and stuffed her body under the floorboards in his living room. Then my mom told me his wife actually left him with two small kids because she wasn't cut out for motherhood. Just up and left for Albuquerque one day with nothing but a note and more responsibility than one man could handle. Divorce papers came a few years later, and by that time, he'd figured out how to raise two kids on his own and run a farm. Never remarried, though. Of course, that was all before I was born because he was old with grown kids in Esperanza by the time I came into the picture. So, I stopped being afraid of him after a time because if my mom of all people said he was a good man, then I believed it.

Anyway, I'm getting distracted. The point of all this was to say that I saved up all that money I'd earned from him and the people he recommended I go to, and I had big plans to do big things with it. Until then, I hid it in under some loose floorboards under my bed—all those lurid tales we made up about old Mr. Consuelo's burying his wife under them got me thinking they would be a good place to hide things. I'd stuffed all that cash under them in a plastic bag and would only pull it out at night and count it all up when my mom was asleep. Then I'd slide it back under the loose planks and crawl into bed and make myself dizzy dreaming up what I would do with all that money the second I got a chance to leave this place behind.

Sherry was the one who had the smarts and the people skills. Me? I was banking on my ability to work hard. It was pretty much all I had going for me.

♦

I guess I should tell you about the time we made a blood pact.

It was one day at the edge of the riverbank right around sunset. The mountains were stained a watermelon pink, and the light was softly streaming through the trees. The summer heat of the day was easing up, and the cicadas were already screeching with the odd cricket struggling to get a word in edgewise.

We shouldn't have been out that late. We knew better, but back then, we were always testing her, trying to prove we weren't afraid of her weeping and wailing. So, we'd hang out by the river right until the sun began to set, and then we'd run home through the Bosque as fast as we could.

Fourteen.

Just old enough to think we knew better and young enough to still hope that there was something beyond this small desert town of Sueño. La Llorona had nothing on two girls with more bravado than sense, or so we liked to think.

The night before, another one had been taken. Laura. A nice enough girl who went to our school. Shy as all get out and better with animals than people. She'd refused to dissect the frogs in science class, even though it caused a big scene, and spent her free time rehabilitating injured wildlife—squirrels who crawled into mouse traps and birds who broke their wings flying into windows. Probably would have made a great veterinarian, but anyway, that was all over now.

We didn't know how it happened, except she must have been by the river when she shouldn't have been, probably trying to rescue one of those injured animals. I could just imagine her chasing after some poor injured otter and then BOOM! down she went into the river and came back up baptized.

The next thing we knew, she showed up to school looking like the rest of them: hair plastered to her skull, hanging in long, wet ropes, her eyes red-rimmed and empty. When it came time to dissect that frog, she didn't even blink, just took the tiny knife and sliced the thing wide open.

The second school was out, and I finished my work for the day, I met Sherry down by the river, running as fast as I could through the cottonwoods and desert olive trees. I found her sitting along the riverbank, throwing stones into the muddy water, probably wishing one or two hit La Llorona.

She looked bold and beautiful in a red polka-dot crop top and daisy dukes. Her long dark hair had been tamed with a curling iron and hung in seductive ringlets that framed her face beautifully in a way I could never get my tangle of black curls to do. She was wearing a new shade of lipstick, a bright pink that didn't really go with her complexion, but I still wanted it, anyway. I looked hot and dusty in my overalls and work boots and hair knotted back in an ugly but serviceable bun. Not for the first time, I wished I was someone who had her style. Course, now I look back and think she was a girl trying to act like a woman, but who wasn't at that age?

We couldn't look at each other at first—it was too hard to see the truth of Laura in each other's eyes. Instead, I watched the geese swimming along the riverbank and the tall grass sway in the soft breeze.

"We can't end up like her," I finally said.

"We won't." She threw that last rock so hard, it scared the birds resting in the middle of a sandbank, and they scattered and took to the sky.

She took an army knife from the back pocket of her shorts and flicked the switch open. "Let's promise each other, right here and now, that we won't ever be like Laura."

It hurt to hear the girl's name out loud, but I knew Sherry said it so we wouldn't be afraid of the thing she'd become. The thing we could become.

"How are we going to make sure we won't?" I asked.

"Blood pact." Then she sliced her palm open.

Forget the futures mapped out for us. Forget what people wanted us to be, and forget that Weeping Woman who lived at the bottom of the river and tried to take us with her. We were powerful women, and we could choose our own fate.

She held out the knife and waited for me to take it. Her other hand was welling with blood, and I stared in horror as it dripped onto the riverbank and snaked its way into the muddy water. She didn't even look like it hurt.

"Nobody can tell us what to do," she said. "Nobody can control our destiny but us."

She looked fierce as she said it, like some low-rent goddess or telenovela starlet at the end of an especially important episode. Not for the first time, I felt she was like some heroine in the sexy books we used to sneak peeks at from the local bookshop. The only things that could get me to part with my precious cash. I would never be that beautiful or that brave.

Sherry was always so strong when I always felt so afraid. In that moment, I believed we could escape our fate. So, I did the scariest thing I'd ever done up until that point in my life, and I took her knife and sliced clear across my own palm. It hurt like a beast, but I refused to cry. My eyes watered something fierce, though.

We held our palms together, and we promised we wouldn't be like our mothers or Laura. That we would protect each other no matter what.

It wouldn't be until later that I realized promises didn't mean a thing.

That night, though? There was magic in our desert air. The sun turned the sky crimson as it set over the mountains in the east and scattered golden diamonds across the river as we made our blood pact.

No sister left behind.

No sister left to the water.

💧

We used to sit along the riverbank and dream up all sorts of things. Telenovela-worthy love affairs and homes so big, they had two stories and a front and back staircase. And fresh flowers every day in the entryway because we could afford to be fancy. Really, what we wanted was assurance that we wouldn't end up like those river women as our chests filled out and we started to bleed.

Somehow our daydreams always ended up on those flowers, though. Sherry wanted those big red roses like the ones they advertised in the paper for Valentine's Day. I liked the wildflowers that grew like weeds across our land, but Sherry said those were for commoners. So, I forgot about them and started thinking about red roses. Those were the kind we'd have in our homes for no reason at all, except they were beautiful and probably from a handsome man that was passionately in love with us.

We knew something like that could be possible for us, however slim the chances, because one time, Sherry's aunt came to visit, and she brought her husband with her. Now Sherry's aunt was one of those women people whispered about because she actually left this small town and nobody, I mean not anybody, thought she would ever come back. She was always the quiet one who refused to two-step on Saturday nights, and worked all the time, and not once did anyone ever see her by the river. Around the time people started calling her a spinster, she packed up and left with all she'd saved from her odd jobs. We used to think about what her life might be like up in the big city of Esperanza and just how great it would be to leave this dustbowl of a town behind.

Anyway, I tell you all this so you can see what a surprise it was to all of us when Sherry's aunt rolled back into town and had a handsome man at her side. He had dark skin and close-cropped black hair that was graying around the temples. Sherry's aunt and him were just about the same height, so when they stood next to each other, you got this strange sense of intimacy, like they could turn and lock lips anytime they wanted. This guy was slim and had the kindest dark-brown eyes. Not once did he wear the clean-cut look of starched shirts and crisp khakis or blue jeans that were stiff enough to chafe when you walked in them. Instead, he wore faded jeans and a simple flannel shirt. He spoke softly and often in Spanish, which was a big deal because that was the forbidden language.

He was a nice match for Sherry's aunt, who was round all over, with hair black and curly like Sherry's, and the soft, floral swing dress she wore accentuating everything that was womanly about her. She had these small, delicate hands—I remember because I couldn't help staring at how those tiny things were cradled in his big, calloused ones, and I figured that was what love must look like.

He was so nice to her! Sherry couldn't wait to tell me all about it, especially the part about how he brought everyone flowers. I didn't believe her until she showed me the bouquets of tiny pink rosebuds dusted with tiny white puffs.

Sherry's mom was going through one of her dry spells—for her, that was a good thing because she spent so much time liquored up that Sherry didn't have much of anyone looking after her. Her mom was trying to get herself together, so the aunt came down to help, though to my knowledge, they never had the best relationship. Maybe it was because Sherry's mom wanted to drown her sorrows, whereas Sherry's aunt wanted to imagine a life where she wasn't defined by them.

"It's baby's breath," Sherry explained as we oohed and aahed over the flowers. "They put it in bouquets to make them look nicer."

She was always so sophisticated and had an answer for everything.

Those pink flowers were just for her, he'd said, and she kept them in a cracked vase on a foldout TV tray that acted as a nightstand, even after they dried up and withered into brown buds. Sherry's mom got petite yellow ones, and Sherry's aunt...well, I almost passed out when I saw her flowers because they were big, fat red roses that practically spilled out of the nice ceramic vase he bought to go with it. They were the kind of flowers that belonged in our two-story houses.

And that's not all. Sherry said her aunt smiled a lot. Smiled! We'd never seen an older woman smile before, so that was something I had to see for myself. So, Sherry invited me for dinner, and over tortillas, chile stew, and beans, we marveled at this quiet, gentle woman and the quiet, gentle man she'd brought with her. It was almost a tragedy to see them in the sad excuse for a home that Sherry and her momma lived in. That place was never clean—I mean, don't think I'm being judgey because my house wasn't much better—it was dirty and falling apart, just like Sherry's mom's.

No amount of cleaning could get the dirt out of the corners, and there wasn't one dish in the house that wasn't chipped. Even the kitchen table we sat around that night was a little wobbly and the chairs a mix of foldouts and poorly mended thrift store finds. Sherry's aunt had tried to spruce things up a bit by washing the windows and curtains, but the light still refused to come in. Sherry's husband was kind enough to ignore what a rundown house it was.

But back to that dinner. The food was exceptionally good, and when I told Sherry's mom so, she laughed and said she didn't cook it. Sherry's aunt's husband had. Sherry and I exchanged looks across the table at that and tried not to let our eyes bulge out of their sockets.

We watched them hold hands under the table, and then after dinner, he got up to help her wash dishes. He got his hands dirty in the dishwater and everything. Without being asked.

Then he did something I'll never forget. He raised his hand to Sherry's aunt, and we instinctively flinched and pulled inside ourselves, waiting for the inevitable smack of flesh.

Only we never heard it.

Instead, standing close to her, he lifted his index finger and swept stray strands of hair from her brow. They gazed at each other and shared a secret smile before he kissed her forehead, nose, lips. The kisses looked soft, like little feathers touching skin.

We'd never seen two people look at each other like that before. We spent the rest of that summer thinking about feather kisses and what it would be like to have a man like that.

Once you know something's possible, the thirst builds up inside you so deep that not even the river can satisfy your cravings. Sherry's aunt told us there were a lot of different ways our lives could go. We just had to figure out how to get out of this damn town.

It was enough to fight the feeling that we should just line our pockets with stones and walk into the river and get things over with. It was enough to start dreaming bigger dreams.

That was when we started to renew our blood pact every year. Our vow that we would never, ever turn out like those others and that we would always protect each other. I was Margarita-Josephina-sometimes-Mercy, and she was Sherry, and we were determined to be better than the rest. The scars on our palms were hard reminders that we couldn't afford not to dream.

By the time we were almost eighteen, we were so close to escaping that we could taste freedom in everything we did. By then, Sherry had scraped enough together to buy her own car. A brown Camaro, which sounds cool but really was so beat up, you couldn't tell it was a cool car, and honestly, it barely ran half the time. But when it did, we cruised it up and down Main Street and drove it through empty lots and sometimes took it out on the highway, though not often, because we never knew when the thing would die on us.

It was ugly as sin, too, but somehow Sherry still made it cool. Me? I was stuck hitching a ride from my momma in her old truck, which I almost never did unless I had to because I didn't want the shame of looking like a child being carted around everywhere. So, I walked to work or got Sherry to drive me, which she did a lot because she wanted people to know she had a car. Hers. Not her momma's or one of her momma's boys, as she called the men her mom was always shacking up with. She paid for it, so nobody could tell her what to do with it.

That was around the time Sherry—you know she was always the smart one—got a full ride to college, and I was figuring out a way to pay for mine. In truth, I wasn't much for sitting at desks and learning more things that didn't seem to be all that useful for my here and now. Maybe I'd just get a job up there somewhere. I'd worked plenty and even figured out how to type up a resume. We could rent an apartment together and do city girl things like we saw on the shows. It wasn't the two-story houses we dreamed of, but it was a start. I had a bundle of cash saved up, so now I just had to figure out what to do with it.

Only one thing was for sure: Together, we would escape this miserable place.

I look back on that fateful night and wish I could have done something. I play it through my mind over and over again. Think about how I could have been a little faster or pushed Sherry a little harder to go home sooner.

But home wasn't a place she wanted to be that night. Her mother's new man had come over. He was drunk as a skunk and went snooping around her room. He was worried Sherry was turning out to be the wrong kind of woman, whatever that meant. I'd rather not tell this part, but the truth was his search led him to her panty drawer and the lacy stuff she kept there. By then, Sherry had gotten pretty good at buying things on super sale or from a five-finger discount, if you get my drift, so she had all this nice sexy woman stuff. Stuff I wished I was pretty enough and brave enough to have and even braver to wear. But I was a coward through and through, and if it weren't for Sherry, I would be no place at all.

Anyway, back to her mom's creepy boyfriend. I look back at it now, and I think there's no reason a grown-ass man should be rooting around in a teenage girl's undies unless he was a pervert, which he was. Anyway, that was how it was then—those kinds of men felt entitled to anything and everyone. He saw those thongs and fancy panties that Sherry cherished and got the wrong idea about who she was riding around with in that car of hers, and up went his hand, and things went from there.

The thing about Sherry was that she only ever showed those panties to me. I mean, I knew for a fact that she wasn't running around with boys because we were both too afraid to try something like that. Like if we did, we'd get pregnant and stuck here. So, we dreamed a lot and hoped a lot and wondered a lot about men like Sherry's aunt's husband. But looking back, I can see we didn't know a damned thing about how things really worked except for what we'd read in books, which wasn't much or all that useful for anything other than dreaming. Anyway, even if she was running around with boys, it was none of that man's business.

I found Sherry walking along the riverbank at sunset, weeping and wailing, her face the color only a hard hand across the mouth can make. She was full of tears. Hot and fat and angry tears, and she wailed—and I told her not to. That's what brings the river woman to you. Our pain is her feast, so I held Sherry and stroked her hair and told her that everything would be all right, but she wouldn't listen.

It hurt to see. Sherry. Sherry Baby, the one who had an answer for everything and had bigger dreams than me, pushed away from my comfort, stalking up and down the riverbank, her hair wild and crazy, wailing that once, just once, she wanted something nice just for her, that nobody could touch unless she told them they could.

She was barefoot and in a pink mini dress that used to be pretty when she'd bought it at a steep discount at the thrift store, but now it was torn and stained and ugly just like her panties were now that the man had put his hands on them. Sherry shouted and cursed that man's name. I hated him just as much as she did, and I wanted him dead.

But I loved Sherry more. I saw the sun setting, and I knew we didn't have much time. If she kept going on like this, La Llorona would come for us for sure. I didn't think Sherry was lucid enough to know she was in danger. I kept talking to her calm and soft, telling her everything was going to be all right and that we should go to my mom's house—I'd stopped thinking of it as home by then—or we could go for a drive, anything, only we couldn't stay here, and she didn't have to go home.

"Sherry, Sherry, we have everything. Three months and we're out of here. Just hold on a little longer, Sherry. Then we can go to the city and live together and figure stuff out where nobody can touch us." Then I went for broke and grabbed her scarred hand in mine. "I still want that big house, but not if you won't live in it with me."

I could tell that got her—Sherry, my Sherry, the brave one who wouldn't take guff from anybody. She was there, that fire in her eyes, just as the sun

slipped behind the mountains and darkness sucked
the life out of the river.

♦

By then, it was too late. We heard her first—the
weeping and moaning like dry desert wind whipping along the riverbank.

Then we took in Sherry's tears, her wild hair, her
bitter spirit. We knew the truth of our situation the
moment we saw a glimpse of a white nightgown in
the distance. That meant she was close—and once
she spotted you, there was no surviving.

There was nothing to do but run.

I don't want to talk about what happened next. I
mean, I don't want to linger on it. What you need to
know is that one minute me and Sherry were side
by side, and the next, I was running alone through
the Bosque.

It was the silence that hit me first. All that weeping
and wailing, then nothing but my heavy breathing,
and something like the sound of leaves being raked
over the earth.

"Sherry? Sherry?" I called out in the darkness.

There was only one place she could be. I thought
of the scar on my palm, the visible promise that we
would never abandon one another. I screwed up all
my courage and got as brave as I could, though I
knew I would never truly be brave, and ran right
back to the river. Back to Sherry and back to the
thing of my nightmares.

I'd never seen her up close before. She wore a
long white dress plastered to her skin, and her hair
was long and wet down her back. You couldn't see

where her feet met the earth. Her skin was as pale as a grub worm's. Her hands were like white spider legs, gripping Sherry by her hair and dragging her to the river.

All the sound came rushing back when I saw them. Sherry was kicking and screaming as La Llorona waded into the water. I called after her and ran right into the river behind them. I grabbed Sherry's hand, could feel the scar along her palm touch mine as I pulled and tugged and tried to get us back on the riverbank. There was screaming and crying and water splashing everywhere.

Then total silence.

♦

Even now, I wrack my brain, trying to figure out how I lost her grip. All I know is that one minute I could feel her hand wrapped around mine, and the next, it wasn't.

"Sherry! Sherry!"

I screamed her name and wished there was some way to see where she went in the darkness. I turned back to the riverbank, hoping she might be dragging herself out of the water. There I was, waist-deep in muddy water, feeling cold and alone and like nothing would ever be the same again.

I was just about to give up hope when I saw something bubble and swirl around me. For a minute, all I could think was it must be Sherry swimming to the surface.

But it wasn't Sherry.

An icy cold hand grabbed my shoulder from behind. Before I knew it, I was under water, thrashing and screaming, and swallowing big mouthfuls of dirty river.

♦

I wish I could tell you how I broke free. I don't rightly know.

It's strange what flashes through your mind when you think it's the end. When you know you're about to be baptized. I mean, I didn't fix on Sherry or my momma or even Sherry's aunt. All I know is that when I thought I was a goner for sure, all I could picture was the sunrise and how I'd miss seeing it each morning. I thought about the hollyhocks, too, growing wantonly along the highway, and the seeds I'd helped Mr. Consuelo plant, the ones I was excited to see burst to life. The way the cottonwoods seemed to wave hello to me every time I walked through the Bosque. And beeswax candles. I would miss the way my kitchen smelled when me and my mom made them to sell for extra cash. Hot and sweet like honey.

Thinking about all that warmth did something to me.

Then, there was this moment. I can't tell you exactly what it was, only that the river was going to take me, and then—I felt La Llorona, well, not let go precisely, but lose her grip a little. Like shrink or become less. Enough for me to jerk loose and flop onto the riverbank like a fish, coughing up river water and gasping for breath.

I wanted to collapse, but I didn't, because I knew if I did, she'd just drag me back. So, I made myself be brave one last time and forced myself up and ran and didn't stop until I cleared the trees, made it through the Bosque—the trees and shrubs seeming to shelter me from La Llorona's gaze—and up my porch steps, not stopping until the door was locked behind me.

I spent the whole night awake, hearing La Llorona raging and weeping because I'd slipped away. Each minute that ticked by was a minute spent wishing Sherry was okay, knowing full well she wasn't.

♦

The next day was my birthday.

I waited all day for Sherry to call, and when the sun set and there was nothing, I knew La Llorona had claimed her. The cake my mother made me that night tasted of wasted life and too much sugar.

We got the recipes from the magazines I read, from places far away from here where they made fancy cakes like Boston cream pie. Which was, I guess, supposed to be a pie and not a cake, which was confusing, but anyway, I got my mother to make it for me. Birthdays were always a little awkward, since it reminded us of the time my dad blew town, so my mom did her best to make a big deal about it, like my birthday wasn't ruined by the memory of him throwing cake in my face.

She didn't ask me about what happened the night before, and I didn't offer up information. She just washed my muddy clothes and hugged me tight at random moments all the next day and made a big fuss over baking that cake. Pie. Whatever. And if she thought I didn't notice her looking at me to see if my eyes were bloodshot or touching my hair at odd moments to see if it was fully dry, well, then she was kidding herself.

It wasn't until I blew out my birthday candles that I realized Sherry was gone. I mean, really gone. She wouldn't show up for cake. I didn't dream up what happened that night or somehow think Sherry was baptized when really she was safe at home all along.

She was never getting out of that river.

♦

I thought I'd survived. The truth ended up being a little more complicated, though it took me a few years and a lot of heartache to work it all out. Sherry showed up a week later. I saw her right outside the diner.

"Sherry! Sherry!" I called out to her, relieved that my friend was once again on dry land. I wanted to know everything. How had she escaped? Why did she miss my birthday? Did she know that Boston cream pie wasn't as great as it sounded?

But I stopped dead in my tracks when I got a good look at her. Her hair was plastered wet against her skull, and her eyes were so dead, you could see the bottom of the river inside them. She wore a dress as ugly and proper as her old ones were garish and loud.

"Sherry?"

the pastor's son—his child from before he became a windower and turned to the priesthood for solace—

She didn't even answer all my stupid questions or hold her scarred palm up to mine—our usual greeting, a reminder that we had the power to change our fates. Instead, she crossed the street and up the steps to the church that stood dead center in the middle of town. The whole time, the only thing I could feel was the damp, clammy hand on my shoulder.

Me? I thought I'd dodged a bullet. But when Sherry wouldn't even acknowledge me, I got so sad and desperate, I could feel it building up inside me like a storm.

🌢

That was the year I turned eighteen. I cried so hard, I caused a flash flood through town that destroyed a lot of property. Thankfully, no one was killed. I was a lot more careful with my tears after that. I bottled my tears up inside myself so I wouldn't hurt anyone. There was no knowing what they could do.

Seeing Sherry like that just about did me in, but it wasn't until I read the wedding bans in the local paper that I broke. There was Sherry, going to marry the pastor's son—his child from before he became a widower and turned to the priesthood for solace—a white stuffed shirt with blond hair and cold blue eyes who looked like the star of a toothpaste commercial but who me and Sherry knew liked to hurt small animals.

Her mother went to live with them, and she'd cleaned up a little, got off the booze, and stopped getting with every man that knocked on her door.

Instead, she turned to God more than I'd ever seen her do before. I thought about writing Sherry's aunt about what happened, but then, I couldn't figure out what I'd tell her. Anyway, she probably already knew. It didn't seem likely she'd ever come back with the way things turned out.

That was when that night on the river became real for me. Until I saw a photo of Sherry and that boy who doesn't even deserve a name in this story, I'd always thought—hoped—that the worst hadn't happened. Sherry was just playing one of her mean tricks, and one day she'd show up on my doorstep in her cutoff jeans and whatever new lipstick shade she was able to lift from the grocery store, asking if I wanted to go hang out by the river.

Those tears burst from me like a dam, and I couldn't control them no matter what I did. My sobs were a violent storm that swept through the town, rattling windows and flooding Main Street and uprooting trees. Afterwards, I noticed that the back of my shirt was soaked through where that river witch had touched me, and then I learned the next day about all the damage I'd caused.

That was when I knew I hadn't gotten away after all.

♦

A year later, my mother passed away. Heart attack, they said, but I knew she died of a broken heart. She'd worked herself to the bone so she wouldn't have to feel all the things she needed to. Her hair grew thinner and grayer like her body until she looked like a small scarecrow in her oversized floral dresses. I think she just gave up one day and stopped holding herself together, and then it was done.

Or maybe it was the secret she kept for so many years that finally did her in. See, I went through her things after she passed and found one of her coffee tins tucked under her bed. Inside was a pile of dirt with something inside it. I pulled it out and found that it was a wallet smashed together with rat bones—don't ask me how I know what rat bones look like—and wrapped in chicken wire.

There was a dark, rusty stain smeared across the top.

Careful not to unwrap the chicken wire—I didn't like the dark, heavy feeling of the inside of the coffee can—I poked along the edges of the wallet enough to see what was inside. I saw a driver's license along with a credit card and a twenty dollar bill.

It was my father's.

No way would he have left town without it. Come to think of it, he never would have left his truck behind either. Suddenly, my mother's dirty fingers and sweat-soaked dress from that night so long ago made sense. So did the fact that my mom was so sure he would never come back. Or how she could never quite get things growing after that.

I don't blame her for what she did.

What choice did she have but to go to La Huesera? I just wish the Bone Woman hadn't taken away the one thing she was good at, but there was always a price for these sorts of things. And now I was going to do my best to do right by her and all that she did for me. I placed the wire-wrapped bones and wallet back into the dirt, sealed the coffee can, put it back under her bed, and went about the business of putting my mother to rest.

I wouldn't bury her in the churchyard. I mean, what did that place ever do for us but give us grief? No, she deserved to be wild and free, so I had her cremated—and boy, did the town talk about that until their jaws hurt from moving—and I spread her ashes around our plot of land. As I did, I wondered why she never did anything with it, I mean before she lost her gift. Everybody said the land was fallow and nothing would grow there, but I looked around and saw wildflowers and tall grass and saltbush. Seemed to me like things were growing just fine.

I wanted to cry, but I couldn't. Not after what happened the last time. It just about broke my heart not being able to grieve my mother properly, but I had to keep people safe, even if they did think badly of me. The last thing I wanted to be was like La Llorona. I held it in as long as I could. When those tears piled up inside me, and I had to let them out, I locked myself in my room. Carefully as I could, I spilled each tear into a mason jar until I was all cried out. I got two jars' worth. Then I curled up in a corner and waited for the worst to happen, staring at my scarred palm and thinking of Sherry.

But nothing did. That was when I learned that I could cry and not hurt people, as long as I contained my tears. As long as they didn't touch the earth.

◆

I got the house and the land it sat on, which made me pretty desirable to the undesirable in town. All sorts of hungry men came out of the woodwork then. I refused their calls and bolted the door against their insistent pounding.

I couldn't choose much in this life, but at least I could choose how I wanted to be moving forward. So, I stayed, and I took a line from Sherry's aunt and never went down to the dance hall on Saturdays and avoided the river when I could, most especially at night. Still, sometimes I got so restless, I had to walk through the Bosque, and there was no separating that wild forest from the Rio Grande that wound through it.

The one thing that stands out to me about this time was how smart my mom was. She set aside money and had things like insurance and the deed to the land and the house. I mean, I was well provided for and had more options than most. That, combined with all the money I'd stuffed under the floorboards, gave me some time to think about my options while I kept working my odd jobs.

So, even though I grew up in an old two-bedroom adobe that was falling apart and never quite clean, I had a mother who gave me a clean slate. She tried to change things in her own way, too, just like I was now, I realized. I guess I wasn't the only one doing just about anything to change my future. I wished she would have told me, and we could have done it together. I was sad for her and the half-life she lived, but I also wanted to do right by what she gave me and thought long and hard about what to do with the land and the money—stashed away in those coffee cans—she'd set aside for me.

Around that time, I got into seeds. I mean, more than I was before. Seemed to me they were perfection in one tiny pod, and they knew that I knew it. We had a good thing going—me, the land, and the seeds. I found a whole stash of them in another one of my mother's tins. Lord, she kept those things everywhere! I didn't think anything would come of it, but I felt like they deserved to be planted. I went out back and spread them across the border of our plot of land and waited and watched all spring to see what would happen. By midsummer, we had the biggest, sweetest wildflowers you ever did see.

♦

I was more vulnerable for being alone. Sometimes it felt as if La Llorona was slowly isolating me, cutting me off from the people I loved, so I had more to weep about and would then be easy pickings. I went on the offensive. I made sure to spend plenty of time in the sun, not afraid to let my skin get nice and brown, knowing full well she preferred pale skin to hide the blemishes of a mixed-race union.

When it wasn't hungry men knocking, it was little kids throwing rocks and triple-dog-daring one another to knock on my door. Witch, they called me. And I didn't blame them. After my mom's sudden passing, Sherry's marriage (a sign of her supposed return to the light), and my own general anti-social behavior, it was easy enough to see me in that way. Especially once you took in the rundown house at the edge of the Bosque. Throw in the fact that they rarely saw me and sometimes heard my lonely cries when I couldn't keep them in, well, the scary story pretty much wrote itself. Okay, and maybe it had something to do with what I did to Sherry's mom, but I'll get to that in a minute. Honestly, I don't know who they were more afraid of, me or La Llorona.

Around that time, my shoulder started aching pretty much nonstop. I could feel her cold, clammy touch on me even in the heat of the day. I couldn't let that stop me, though. The only time it seemed to let up was when I was doing something I loved. I kept filling my flower garden in the front of the house with morning glories and hollyhocks and dandelions because I knew she hated anything that shamelessly grew, wanton in their desire to thrive.

♦

After a while, I counted up all the dollars and coins my mom and I had saved and took them to the bank to start my own account, official and everything. Mr. Consuelo was kind enough to go with me to make sure those boys didn't harass me. By then I'd learned to trust him—my mom had told me a few months before she'd died that he was one of the few men who was actually in love with his wife and never got over her breaking his heart and leaving. From what I'd seen of him, it fit, so I knew he wouldn't ever try anything hinky with me, so I asked for his help. I'd done the research and knew what I had to do to open an account, but I also knew that I didn't have the best reputation around town. I wished my mom had taught me how to do these things, but there was no helping that now. There was no way they'd let me invest all this money without trying to take it for themselves. Things were different back then and, Sueño being a small town, they could pull one over on me if I wasn't careful. I could just see them making up stuff about me stealing it—they were that mean. So, Mr.

Consuelo was there to make sure they didn't try any funny business.

He let me do things myself, though, which I appreciated. He just sat right next to me as quiet and solid as the earth while I filled out the paperwork and got things going. He gave the paperwork a thorough once-over, not because he didn't trust me to know what I was about but to make sure those boys knew that he was looking out for me. You could call it sexist. Say they had no right to defer to a man like that when I was a grown woman with a good head on my shoulders, and you would be right. But I wasn't about to talk sense to idiots because I knew it wouldn't change a damn thing. So, I let Mr. Consuelo be the big man who protected me while I signed the paperwork, handed over my plastic bags of cash and coins, and that was that.

After, over celebratory lemonade, I talked to Mr. Consuelo about what I might be able to do with the land out back, and he was kind enough to take a look at things for me. Sure enough, the earth was ready for planting. I even had access to the acequias and water rights. Water rights alone would be reason enough for a man to attach himself to a woman who had them. The house was a dump, but land and water rights? Those things were pure gold in the middle of a desert. That was why I spent so much time chasing people off in those days. My mother gave me this, and nobody was going to take it away from me.

The thing is, even though Mr. Consuelo helped out, knowing full well what that town thought of me, he never held it against me or tried to be the man of the house like I'd seen so many men try to do when they saw a woman on her own. He just helped out as he could, the same way he let me help out around his farm as a kid. I look back and think that he was always kind. I wished he knew how much I appreciated it, though I'm sure he did, especially after he hired me on as his farm manager, so I could make enough to keep my head above water and still keep saving.

Then I started thinking about what to do with all that land.

♦

I thought of moving away, sure. But I knew she would find me. The second I let my guard down, she would be there in the street puddles and dishwater. I'd rather stay where I knew the playing field. If I hadn't been marked then, sure, I could be like Sherry's aunt and leave everything behind, but that was too late for me. A bunch of roads closed for me that night on the riverbank, so I had to choose from the few paths available to me. And anyway, I liked to keep La Llorona where I could see her.

Plus, I couldn't leave Sherry. She'd gotten pregnant but still couldn't carry a baby to term, like her body was rejecting passing down this legacy. She still wouldn't talk to me and always crossed the street when she saw me coming her way, but somehow, I felt it was important to be there for her. I left her care packages when I could, and as far as I knew, she used them, because when I came to leave something else, the basket was empty and waiting by her back door.

It wasn't much, but it gave me hope.

◆

I thought I might invest in some chickens and sell their eggs so I'd have another income stream in addition to my role as farm manager while I figured out what to do with the house and the land. I built the chicken coop and bought the chickens, and things went all right for a week or two. Then that stupid water witch came in the night and ripped those poor birds to shreds. I woke up the next morning after a severe thunderstorm to blood and feathers and guts everywhere. After a few hours mucking things out, I knew selling eggs wouldn't work. It wasn't fair to the chickens. She wouldn't stop with just the few I had.

People said it was a coyote, but I knew better.

I did find one egg left in the corner of the coop that hadn't been touched by her wet, greedy hands. I didn't much feel like eating it, but I didn't want it to go to waste after so much had been lost. I went inside, put on some coffee, and set about making breakfast. I thought that egg was a miracle until I cracked it over my skillet, and it came out with a blood-red yolk that crackled and sizzled under the heat. That put me off eggs for a good long while.

◆

After the chickens, she got in the habit of leaving little presents for me. One day a dead squirrel, another the upturned roots of a cottonwood in the middle of my favorite walking path, the next, a rock through my window. The stray cats knew something was off and wouldn't step foot on my property and I was glad about it. I didn't want any more animals getting hurt on my account. She didn't like anything to grow, and she hated that I managed to go about my daily routine, despite her handprint seared into my shoulder.

That's okay. I hated her, too. And it was with that fire that I could heat my stove at night and have enough strength to hold in all my tears until I was safe at home and could cry comfortably into a large mason jar. She did what she did to me. I couldn't change that. But that didn't mean I had to go inflicting it on others. One day, I would be strong enough to face her. I would baptize her like she tried to baptize me. I would grab her and force her face-first into the water and steal her tears, so she had nothing to keep her afloat. She would drown, of course, and get sucked up by the hungry soil at the bottom of the riverbank. These were the dreams that fueled me now, vases full of red roses in big houses a thing of the past.

♦

The next time I cried, I killed someone.

I'd been walking down Main Street with a paper bag overloaded with supplies from the hardware store. Vandals had spray-painted my front door again and knocked down part of my fence, so I was getting what I needed to fix things up. I'd had to park a ways away, and all my focus was going into reaching my truck before the whole bag burst open. I should also admit that I was in a pisser of a mood because the cashier there, a mean old lady who looked like she sucked on lemons for fun, was going out of her way to be cruel. Hinting that I was no good and that ladies didn't wear overalls, and there must be something wrong with me if I wasn't married by now.

She was angry at me, of course, because her son had been one of the boys knocking on my door a few years back, and I had rejected him along with the rest. She took it personally, offended that anybody could ever think themselves too good for that nose picker. So, that mean old woman overfilled my bag on purpose because she wanted to see me struggle down the street. That's how things were back then. People wouldn't come right out and do bad things—they saved that stuff for the privacy of their homes. But they would mutter under their breath and whisper and do passive-aggressive things like overstuff your bag, knowing it was likely to break any second. They liked to find little ways to make you suffer and, at the same time, say things like *God bless you* after you sneezed.

Anyway, I was walking down the street and feeling tired and worn down and just angry with this town's casual meanness. I saw Sherry's mom right outside the liquor store in a Sunday dress, handing out religious pamphlets and mini bibles. My truck was parked right in front, so there was no avoiding her.

I stopped dead in my tracks. She looked cleaned up, but nothing could soften the years of hard boozing written across her face. Her skin was gray and sallow like the life got sucked out of her. The thing about Sherry's mom was that she'd never been a mean woman. Not outright, anyway. Her hurtfulness came from looking the other way when the men in her life did as they pleased. Like the time me and Sherry were around ten, and one of her beaus smacked my ass hard and said it wouldn't be long until I turned into a woman worth looking at. He said Sherry was already looking like a woman, and he gave her a once-over that made my skin crawl. Me and Sherry waited that day for her mom to say something or to kick him out of the house. But she never did. She just looked out the window over the kitchen sink and went about washing dishes. Back then, Sherry's mom was always looking the other way. That was why Sherry spent most of her time at my house.

So, there I was, holding on to that paper bag for dear life when she looked at me with those dead eyes, held out a pamphlet, and said, "Jesus loves you."

I waited for her to recognize me, but I don't think she knew who I was, or maybe she'd just forgotten that her daughter once had a friend named Mercy. Then my bag burst open, and I cursed a blue streak. Sherry's mom clutched the cross around her throat at my colorful language and just watched me struggle to pool the contents of my bag together. There were a few people walking up and down the street, and not one of them bothered to help me pick up my stuff.

"You are in pain, mi'ja, but the good Lord loves you and will save your immortal soul."

I looked up, and Sherry's mom was holding out one of those small bibles. I guess my situation was dire enough to upgrade from the pamphlets to the good book in her estimation and worrisome enough for her to let the forbidden language slip out.

I lost it.

"What has the Lord ever done for me?" I yelled. "Take your stupid bible and choke on it!"

Then I took that stupid little bible and threw it right back in her stupid face. It bounced off her forehead, but she just clutched her cross some more and started praying.

"Pray all you want," I told her. "Doesn't make you a better person."

I started scooping up my supplies and throwing them in the back of the truck, broken bag be damned, and drove off with her and half the town glaring at me. When I got back home, I just sat in my truck for a minute and tried to calm myself, but I was so angry, then sad at what an awful woman Sherry's mother was.

See, I'd been thinking. Maybe Sherry hadn't lost her grip in the water. Maybe she'd let go. Maybe she was so tired of dealing with her drunk mother and those creepy "uncles" that she couldn't take it anymore and just wanted it to be over with. So maybe it wasn't my fault. If what happened to Sherry was anyone's fault, it was her mom's. She was the one who never protected her. The one who brought all those bad men in, and the one who didn't even notice when Sherry's running off to my house was the only thing that kept anything bad from happening to her at night. More than the beatings, I mean.

I thought about how terrible Sherry's mom was, and I kept wishing she would pay for all those times she looked away. I mean, really suffer. She deserved to die for taking Sherry's future before she could even have one. And as I was thinking all those ugly thoughts, a few tears slipped out and fell on my lap before I could contain them.

The next day, Sherry's mom was dead. Choked to death on a turnip.

I can't say I was sorry.

◆

Anyway, that's how I solidified the reputation of being a witch. I mean, I see how they thought that. We get in this big fight, and the next day, BAM! she turns up dead.

That was also when I learned I had to be careful with my thoughts. I absolutely had to contain those tears, or something bad would happen. It was one thing to unleash a flood accidentally when I didn't know any better, but it was another thing entirely to will someone dead. I should have been afraid. I should have gone back for one of those mini bibles and been worried for my soul or terrified I was becoming like La Llorona. But I wasn't.

For one, it felt good to get rid of Sherry's mom. She was a bad woman, and I was tired of pretending she wasn't. I was tired of being blamed for the bad things the town kept locked behind closed doors. I'm not saying she wasn't to be pitied—nobody asked for the blows life gave her—but she didn't have to pass that on to her daughter or take it out on me. I'll never forgive her for either of those things, and I don't regret choking her to death with her own tears.

I know. I said it was a turnip. But the truth is, it was her own sorrow that really killed her because that was all I could think about when I was crying, imagining it bubbling up inside of her until it filled up her throat and lungs and her heart stopped. She was everything I hated about Sueño, and I wanted her out of my life and out of Sherry's life. Still, that was a lot of power to have, so I didn't want to go around killing people willy-nilly.

Sherry's mom was a special case.

As for everything else, I realized after that incident that I could control my tears. I mean, I literally poured my will into them and made things so. I wasn't sure how I felt about that and decided to keep crying into the mason jars just to be safe.

The thing is, getting rid of Sherry's mom like that didn't make me feel closer to La Llorona, though I did understand how good it felt to control people's fates like she did. It felt like I was stamping out a weed. I liked that feeling but wasn't sure that I liked that I liked it.

In any case, I couldn't stop thinking about turnips after that, so I bought some seeds and planted them.

♦

One time, La Llorona burned my house down. Violent monsoons swept through the riverbank and the Bosque, and she used the lightning to strike my home and burn it to the ground. That fire burned hot and fierce so that everything inside was reduced to ashes, everything except the tin can that held my father's wallet wrapped in chicken wire, which I'd buried at the front of my property about a month before. I didn't like it in the house and I had a feeling it might do more than just keep one bad man away. There was a powerful energy to it and my mom had given up a lot for it, so I buried it along my property line hoping it would protect me and my land from

men like my father. Anyway, back to La Llorona
burning down my house.

I think she was trying to hurt me. In truth, she did
me a favor.

The walls had been crumbling and the timber
bucking for some time, plus the rooms were full of
so much sadness that it was like an ugly perfume
each time I walked inside. That was why I spent
most of my time outdoors, either trying to figure out
what to do with my land or at Mr. Consuelo's farm
keeping things running.

But then La Llorona burned that life to the ground
and watched from her watery bed, waiting for me to
burst into tears and commit myself to the river.

Only I didn't cry.

Didn't shed one tear. Instead, I called the insurance company and got enough money to build a
new adobe home with enough left over to take all
those seeds I'd been collecting and finally do something official with them. The money my mother and
I had stashed away in the house had been safely
tucked away in the local bank by then, which made
me grateful I'd finally worked up the gumption to
walk into those polished doors and open an account a few years back. So, I had plenty of money
to figure out a new life for myself.

I was bold, too.

I thought long and hard about what I wanted to
do with the insurance and the money I'd saved up. I
insisted on a bigger house than the one I came from
and got a loan for what the insurance didn't pay for,
with Mr. Consuelo's backing. I'd decided that one
day I did want a family—when it was safe—so I built
a nice adobe with two stories and a few rooms that
would keep us warm in the winter and cool in the

summer. I made sure I was careful with expenses because those builders would nickel and dime you if you weren't smart about things, especially if you looked young and green like I did at the time. Then I set about turning the land around it into something productive. I'd decided that the only way I could make that future real was by planning for it now.

That was how Mercy Farm came to be.

♦

I know, I know. Sherry would roll her eyes at the name, but the truth is, I wasn't a Margarita or a Josefina. I was a Mercy, and there was no outrunning my name any more than I could outrun that witch at the bottom of the river. I would make my name beautiful, just like I would make this land beautiful. Just like I could now smile a big, beautiful smile every time I thought of La Llorona raging when she realized what a gift she'd given me by burning my past to the ground.

The thing is, I realized my mom had a lot of money—like a lot. I mean, what was a lot for us back then. Enough for me to build a new house and invest in a new farm with the help of that little loan, what I'd earned myself, and careful planning. So, it struck me one day to wonder why she didn't do anything with all that money. I mean, we could have had a better life together.

Maybe all her energy just went into keeping her heart together, and she didn't have space for anything else. Or maybe her future was taken from her the night she went to La Huesera. Who was I to judge? Then, I thought of all the books I threw away that made me happy. I realized that once you got used to living a certain way, you stopped trusting the good things that happened, even if you made it so.

There was only one thing to do with a revelation like that. I got serious about my farm. It wasn't about planting some stray seed my mom had collected anymore. I talked to old Mr. Consuelo about farming and did a bunch of research for the best way to go about things. I learned the land, tilled the soil, and did all the things you're supposed to do to get a good crop. I read up on square foot gardening and regenerative organic agriculture and adapted some of those practices so I could make the most of the space I had, since my land was only a handful of acres. Not quite big enough to be a proper farm, according to some. It would help me save on water and maximize my yield all while utilizing the natural ecosystem to help with stuff like pest management and soil regeneration. I'd grown up working on various properties, including Mr. Consuelo's, so I had a fairly good sense of how things worked.

He introduced me to the farmers' group and some of the CSA people, so I had contacts established when the time came to sell my produce—I won't get into all that since it's not central to this story. What I will say, though, since we're on the topic, is that there were some real bastards in those groups like I expected. But there were also more men like Mr. Consuelo, and some good women, and it was a nice thing to see. Some of them I already knew from working on their land all those years. They looked out for me, and I got used to going to meetings and arguing about water rights and doing all the stuff you're supposed to do when you're part of a community of farmers. I'd never run in circles like that before—where people looked out for you, even if there were a bunch of bad apples in the bunch—and I liked knowing this town had more than perverts, abusers, and morons in it.

Mr. Consuelo was a big help, and he seemed happy that I was doing something with all the things I learned from him. He even hinted from time to time that I might consider buying his land and making Mercy Farm bigger, but I didn't have that kind of money. I mean, the money my mom saved up felt like a magical gift, but this wasn't a fairy tale, and that windfall wouldn't go on forever.

I started with turnips, then radishes, beets, and lettuces. When they were doing well, I decided to expand to corn, squash, and beans. If they were good enough for my ancestors, they were good enough for me. Tomatoes came next, and after a while, I liked to think Mercy Farm was building a nice reputation for delicious produce at affordable prices. At least, people said my food was good and clean.

That was the word they used because I didn't use pesticides or other junk that would hurt the earth. I used natural pest control methods and a water-efficient irrigations system and listened to the land. We got into a few arguments now and then, me and the land, mostly when I tried to make it do what I wanted. But most of the time, it just told me what it needed, and I listened and did what it said. Things worked out better when I did.

When I had enough produce, I went once a week to the city—Esperanza, it was called, did I mention that earlier?—for their big growers' market, and usually had my stock wiped out by the end of the day. I couldn't technically call my produce organic because it cost a small fortune to get certified, and Mr. Consuelo said it wasn't worth the time or money. But I did explain that I used sustainable and earth-friendly practices, which was all that my customers seemed to care about.

I did a lot of the work myself in those days because it was hard to find trustworthy workers. I mean, people who wouldn't hurt me or try to steal my land—I was still getting used to the idea that I was safe, at least safer than I was growing up, and better protected because of La Huesera's tin can spell guarding my land now. The work was okay because I was young and had an aching shoulder that reminded me the only thing keeping me from the bottom of the Rio Grande was this farm. I didn't sleep much either, and found a bone-deep satisfaction in making things grow.

Most weeks, I put enough aside from my harvest to add to the baskets I left for Sherry on her husband's back porch. I filled it with different things week to week but always made sure she got a bundle of those tasty turnips.

♦

So, I got myself a new house next to the Bosque with some farmland behind it. Don't ask me how I was able to do all that with a little nest egg and some insurance. It's not worth going into all the details and the how-so's because this isn't that kind of story. All I can say was that my mother did a good thing when she left me that money, and I did a good

thing when I spent all my extra time learning the
value of hard work.

I wasn't going to waste my chance. Still no marriage—like I said, I was determined to wait until
the curse was broken or until I met someone who
would break it with me. In the meantime, I learned
to walk around puddles, make quick use of the toilet, and never linger near the opening of the pipes
when it was my turn to water my crops from the
acequias. Even my dishes needed to be washed
quickly because La Llorona tried to reach out to me
any way she could, even through my kitchen sink.
Wherever I went, her presence was an eerie lullaby,
like the song named after her.

More years passed, and I got used to how my
life was going to be. Don't ask me how old I was
by then. I'm not going to tell you because I wish
people would just stop asking me about why I'm
not married already, and why I let myself get so old
before catching a man, as if a man were a type of fish
I could reel in, stuff, and mount above my fireplace.
What I will say is that thirty could be a number I was
getting used to seeing, but that's the most you'll get
out of me. I won't tell you which side of that number
I was on. And anyway, I never really celebrated my
birthday anymore, so what did it matter?

Maybe the little crow's feet starting to appear
around my eyes gave things away a bit, but I figured
if I was still young enough to have kids, then that
was all that mattered. And don't go telling me about
how women are conditioned to want those things.
I know more than most how we're told what we
should want. But that—children, a marriage free
from that curse—that was all me. I felt it deep in

my bones and knew it had nothing to do with what people told me I should be pining for.

At night, when it was cold and lonely and the revenge fantasies stopped soothing me, I thought of Sherry's aunt and a man who would tuck my loose hair behind my ears.

It was enough to keep me going.

When I was so alone I thought I might die, I got a public library card. That was one winter when there was less to do around the farm, even with my cold weather plants I still grew using covers across parts of my field that would mimic a greenhouse. I made beeswax candles in the colder months, grew some things, repaired what needed repairing, but mostly had too much time to myself. So, I read a lot and learned a lot. And finally, I got old enough that the men in the town stopped trying to knock on my door and went in search of younger women. Girls, really. The bad ones went for the ones touched by La Llorona and the good...well, I haven't met any of them yet, except maybe Mr. Consuelo and a few others around his age, which did me no good in the romance department.

When the farm was up and running and things were quiet for a while, he told me he was moving up to Esperanza to be close to his children and grandkids. It made sense. Mercy Farm was doing so well, I didn't have to manage his farm anymore, and he was getting on in years. He had always been close with his kids. We'd gotten close, too, over the years, and not a day went by when he didn't go on about that family of his. I could tell he wanted to know them better beyond the regular visits up north. I liked the idea for him, too, and hoped he'd find someone up there to hold at night. Nobody deserved to go through this life alone.

He wanted to sell me the farm, only I didn't have a ton of money left after building a new house and investing in my land. Plus, I didn't know what to do with it all by myself. So, he put a "For Sale" sign up, and I promised to look in on the property from time to time. He insisted on giving me his tractor before he left, though.

It was a smaller one and came with attachments that would help me till my raised beds and drive around the property as needed. He often loaned it to me anyway when I needed to do a big harvest, and it didn't get in the way of his own work.

I told him I couldn't, and he said, "Please. Your mother...I promised I'd look after you, is all."

It occurred to me then that kind old Mr. Consuelo, probably the only nice man I'd known personally, had been keen on my mother. Keen in a sweet way, like in an *if I were twenty years younger* kind of way. He'd been pining for a long time and knew nothing would ever come of it. Can you blame him? My mom was a looker, even when she was wasting away. But with all she went through, she wouldn't be likely to let another man in, let alone an older one.

Though now that I think about it, Mr. Consuelo would have been a good one. I mean, now that I knew he hadn't actually killed his wife. That man had a good heart. He certainly helped me out more than any neighbor ever should, and he cared more about his kids more than I'd ever seen any man in town do, once he got to talking about them. And I'm pretty sure he did see me all those years ago sneaking onto his property and hiding behind his trees and let me have my sanctuary.

So, I took the tractor and promised to look in on the place until it sold. I also thought long and hard about him finding someone he could share his life with. He deserved more than unrequited love. I teared up a little thinking about it but didn't let them fall. The last thing I wanted to do was hurt a man as good as Mr. Consuelo.

When he left, things got quiet and a little lonely. I tried to take comfort in the feral cats, roadrunners, and other wild animals that started visiting my farm, but I didn't let myself get too close to them. I didn't want La Llorona tearing them to bits like she did those chickens. But it wasn't the same thing as having someone to talk to. I don't think I realized how much I depended on him for basic human contact, let alone basic human kindness. Still, he sent me letters from time to time, and I stuck them on my fridge and got on with things around the farm.

La Llorona still wept and moaned and kept me from my sleep most nights. That was where those library books came in—those words drowned out her noise and helped me hear myself think. I was finally getting to a place where I knew my thoughts were my own, and that my feelings were my own, and my heart was my own. Not hers, not anybody else's. Just mine. It was hard work. I'd say harder than working the land from dawn 'til dusk each day, but that would be overstating things.

I wanted to get her out of my life, that was for sure. But I couldn't do that until I was strong enough. So, I woke up at dawn, when her power waned, every morning of every week of every year since the day she marked me, and tended my land. The droughts had been getting harder and harder each year, making stones out of seeds and hard hearts out of too many hopes dashed to bits. But I was determined to see Mercy Farm thrive.

I was reborn with the sun and the earth and the seeds in my hands.

♦

I went to Main Street once for supplies and ran into Sherry at the grocery store. I hated to see Sherry like that. Beaten and empty, like a burlap sack without the pinto beans. This was around the time her husband had given up on her producing children—okay, a son—and took his anger out on her with his fists, and his nights were spent with some other woman he knew from his church work.

I had been mindlessly strolling through the aisles, thinking what I really ought to do was make a grocery list so I wouldn't waste so much time thinking about what I might need when I went into town for supplies. In truth, I enjoyed grocery shopping. It was exciting to look at new things. Even though I didn't buy much, I enjoyed getting away from the farm and thinking about the kind of life you saw in all the home magazines on display at the front of the store. Plus, I wouldn't say no to air conditioning with this blistering summer heat. August had only just started, and already the land was half-scorched from drought and heat. I found myself looking forward to the fall something fierce.

I'd talked myself into buying a few fashion magazines because the farm was doing well despite the heat, and I was feeling fine. I was thinking all these thoughts, wondering if I should go back and buy those discount plates with daisies on them to add to my kitchen, when I rounded the corner and stopped dead in my tracks.

Sherry stood in the middle of the makeup aisle. A wet braid hung down her back and her dress—buttoned up to her neck and reaching past her ankles—looked stuffy and like a terrible thing to wear on a hot summer day. I could see the yellowed bruise peeking out from her collar.

"Sherry?" I called to her but could tell she didn't hear me, so I slowly rolled my cart up right next to her to see what she was staring at so hard.

The lipstick rack. My eyes hit on what used to be her favorite color: Seduction Red. It was the deep satin of a hot romance and used to look good on her. I mean, she was smokin' when she wore it.

"Sherry, you okay?" I asked again.

She turned to me with those dead, red-rimmed eyes and took in my dusty overalls and wild hair and my cart full of magazines, bread, shampoo, tampons, a new shaver, and a bunch of other stuff I couldn't grow or make myself. We were both older, our faces sharper without the baby fat. I knew I was no spring chicken, but Sherry looked more weathered than me, for all she stayed indoors and I worked on the farm. But I could still see the old Sherry underneath, though I wasn't sure she knew who I was. She didn't say one thing, just clutched the cross resting against her collar and looked at me the way all those other prissy church ladies did, and walked away.

That was the closest I'd been to Sherry in a number of years. It stung to see her reject me like that, even though I knew it wasn't her but the river witch. For a moment, looking at lipstick, I thought Sherry, the real Sherry, might come back. That's the thing with being hopeful. You set yourself up for disappointment.

I stood in front of that lipstick display for a few more minutes before adding a tube of Seduction Red to my cart and heading toward the checkout. I felt mighty frivolous with my items and could tell the checkout lady was judging me when she bagged those magazines and the lipstick. She could barely deal with the tampons—those were for sluts who didn't have any virtue left to protect, while good girls used pads—but when she saw that tube of red lipstick, well, I just knew tongues would be wagging all over town about me. Again.

I knew what she was thinking. It's not like I didn't hear the whispers. The stuff people said about me now that me and Sherry were no longer friends, and my momma was dead, and Sherry's momma was dead, and I'd chased all those men away, and I'd stopped going to church. Shrew. Spinster. Witch. Whore. Now, that last one got me because I didn't get how you could be both a spinster and a whore, but that's small-town logic for you. In any case, buying red lipstick meant I was a whore for sure. I mean, think of all the men I'd be wearing it for!

I tried not to take it personally. They were just afraid. They didn't know what to think about me, so they thought the worst. It gave me a whole new understanding of Sherry's aunt, and how strong she must've been to withstand all that malice coming at her for all those years. It still stung, all the more because I'd realized that I hadn't thought about Sherry for weeks, maybe even months, until I ran into her in the makeup aisle. Even dropping off her weekly basket of produce had become so routine, I'd let the whole reason behind it slip from my mind. It made me feel terrible, guilty, like the kind of guilt I only felt when I used to go to church.

This time, I did cry. I couldn't help it. I was careful, though. I held it in until I got home and dragged my groceries inside. Then I took one of the empty mason jars I stored under the sink for just such an occasion and sat down at my kitchen table for a good long sob. I made sure each tear spilled into the jar. It took some time because I only let one out at a time, but by the end of it, the jar was full, and I felt better. I sealed it up tight once I was done and stuck it in my pantry along with the other jars full of tears. There it was: over a decade's worth of sorrow and pain. They took up most of the back shelves now, and not for the first time, I wondered what I was supposed to do with all of them, as I was beginning to run out of space.

When I was done, I unloaded my groceries and put the magazines on my coffee table. Then I went into my room and sat in front of my vanity. It was more of an old wooden desk with a mirror over it that I'd bought for a song at the Esperanza Growers' Market a few years back. It reminded me of one of those vanities you read about in books, though mine wasn't nearly as fancy and was really sort of impractical, given my line of work. Still, it made me feel like I was more than seeds, freckles, and spinsterhood. I bought it and filled it with things that made me feel nice, like lotions, a silver comb, and sometimes stones or crystals strung up on leather that I'd started collecting, though I had little enough use for those things.

I placed the tube of Seduction Red lipstick on the vanity and stared at it for a long time. I thought about trying it on, but I didn't have it in me to break the seal. So, I stuck it in the drawer and tried to forget all about it.

It wouldn't have looked good on me, anyway.

♦

One time, I was feeling mighty fine and thought I'd try something different. I saw this ad in a magazine where a woman was in an obscenely large bathtub and covered up to the neck in bubbles. This was in a room with a marble floor, and there were candles everywhere, and she had her hair up all nice and a face mask on. Well, I got to thinking a nice long soak after a hard day's work would be nice.

This was a few months after my run-in with Sherry, and I was trying hard to let myself enjoy things more. It occurred to me after seeing her that her fatal flaw was not believing that her future was right in front of her. Or maybe she was too afraid to take it with both hands. I began to wonder if we didn't hold back and do half the work for La Llorona with all that we ran from life.

So, I bought some bubble bath and made more beeswax candles and set about having myself a spa night. I mean, my bathroom was nowhere near as nice as the one in the picture. My tub was only long enough for me to sit upright and was right next to the toilet, but I made do.

It was lovely. I mean, divine! I could see why fancy women liked this. I put on the radio, and the music was soft and sweet, like the candlelight against the fading day. I was so relaxed, that I was about to fall asleep in that tub.

That was when I felt cold hands grip the soles of my feet and pull me under. I should have seen it coming. Why willingly linger in a body of water? But I didn't, and that was how I found myself drowning in bubbles and thrashing around in my tub. It's also how I learned that evil woman could find me any-where—and I mean anywhere—so I could never let my guard down.

Her grip was strong. Seemed like the harder I fought, the stronger she got. I was flailing about, my arms searching for anything and everything to hold on to when I knocked one of those beeswax candles into the tub. To this day, I have no idea why that scared her, but it did. She recoiled something quick at the hiss of the flame when the wax hit water.

I didn't waste a second—I hoisted myself out of the tub and collapsed on the bathroom floor, choking and sputtering and sopping wet. Took me forever to clean up the mess and cough up all those flower-scented bubbles. My feet were cold and sore for days, with claw marks where her bony fingers hooked into my skin.

Whoever said bubble baths were relaxing was a big fat liar.

◆

Late the next winter, some city boy bought Mr. Consuelo's land next door. I got a postcard from Mr.

Consuelo telling me about it before the "Sold" sign showed up in front of the property. It was strange seeing signs of life there after I'd gotten used to living without the old farmer. I checked in from time to time until the paperwork was signed and the new owner took over. Never in all my life did I think someone would ever take over that plot of land that had been sitting there empty for a few seasons, house as pretty as a picture, land as wild and rugged as my own. But he did.

Anyway, it was a lot of noise at first over there as they aired out the house and cleaned up some of the land to get it ready for planting. Then quiet. I figured that had nothing to do with me, so long as he kept to his side of the fence. I forgot about him until one day in the early spring when La Llorona got to me, and I couldn't break free on my own.

I was taking a pre-dawn walk in the Bosque after it had rained long and hard the night before. I hadn't slept all that well because La Llorona whipped up that storm and threw hard pellets of rain at my window and screeched and howled for me to come out to her. I didn't, but that didn't stop her from trying. In the morning, I looked outside to see tree branches scattered all over my land, and plants crushed and drowned by the storm. It was a little too much to take in after all the work I'd put in getting the spring planting done.

So, I went for a walk to clear my head. Nothing I could do until the land dried out a bit, anyway.

Okay, that's not entirely true. Well, I was bummed that she tore up my land, but that was nothing new. The fact was I was feeling a little blue because it was the anniversary of Sherry's baptism. And the next day would see me another year on the wrong side of thirty. It brought everything back. That night. The cold, wet mark on my shoulder, my mother's passing a year later. What terrible things birthdays are. All the ugly little details of my past filled up my head until I couldn't see straight. I was trying hard not to cry, so I figured a walk would help me clear my head.

But all it did was bring me closer to that Weeping Woman. The cottonwoods, the saltbushes, even the little paths winding through the Bosque reminded me of Sherry, and all those feelings started to well up inside of me, daring me to cry. Even the rain-soaked earth and scattered storm debris made me think of her soul at the bottom of the river. So, I walked faster and faster until I was practically running, and didn't stop until I felt water pooling around my ankles.

That woke me up out of my frenzied thoughts. I looked down and saw I'd walked right into the swollen river. The sun wasn't quite up yet, and there was that early morning hush that only happens after a violent storm.

Of course, you know what happened next. I felt her pulling me into the mud until there was dirty water in my nostrils, and my arms were flailing as I tried to brace myself against the wet sediment. That's how the river gets when it's fat with rain. It floods the Bosque, and the ground near the river gets loose and wet like quicksand and will suck you up like it's nothing.

I knew it wasn't nothing.

It was La Llorona. I fought and kicked and tried to scream, but she just filled my mouth with muddy water, her long, bony fingers raking my arms as she tried to force me deeper into the water. This was

it. I was a goner for sure, I figured, though I kept
flailing and fighting and refusing to give up. Here I'd
been fighting her all these years, only to be foolish
enough to go walking along the river before the sun
was fully up and fall under her spell. I suddenly had
a lot more empathy for those stupid girls who didn't
realize what they were getting into, walking along
the riverbank at night like it was just a riverbank.

Then I felt two big hands on my shoulders. Warm
and firm, and before I knew it, I was out of the
water with my ass on solid ground. I was coated in
mud and spent a few good minutes coughing and
sputtering, while those big warm hands slapped my
back to force out all the dirty water from my lungs.
Then those hands held my chin, and I felt a soft
cloth across my face, wiping the mud away.

When I opened my eyes, I saw what looked
like an angel. Dawn had broken. Sunlight streamed
through the trees behind him and made him look
like he was surrounded by a halo. But that could
have been the lack of oxygen talking.

He was dark and looked like he wasn't afraid of
the sun or the Lord. He didn't look like he was
afraid of the word Indian either. He had long, black
hair that hung just past his wide shoulders, and he
didn't seem to care what anyone thought about that.
He had a sort of rough look but in a nice way, like
maybe he broke his nose in a bar fight but also knew
what soap was. He had two small tattoos, one on the
inside of each wrist, which must have been painful
to get, though I couldn't make out what they were.

I know what you're thinking: Why would a
woman with my history be attracted to someone
who so obviously seemed rough and like he was up
to no good? But it was more like with the broken

nose and the tattoos, I knew that he wasn't hiding who he was, not like the clean-cut church guys who were smooth as butter up front and saved their cruelty for behind closed doors. This man was who he was and wasn't about to hide it. That's what I liked about him.

"You okay?" he asked.

I shook my head, and when I tried to talk, it came out like a squeak.

"Here, have some water," he said and handed me his water bottle.

I did and cleared my throat some more. "What happened?"

"I was walking, and I wasn't paying attention to where I was going, and I slipped and fell." That was mostly true. "It happened so fast."

"Don't you know you have to be careful along the river? Especially after a rain like this."

Now, I could have laughed at that because if anyone knew it wasn't safe to walk along the river, it was me. But I saw his point, and I knew he didn't know the whole story, and I wasn't about to educate him on matters. So, I shrugged and drank more water.

"Can't you swim?"

I shrugged. "Never learned."

He looked like he wanted to scold me but thought better of it. "Well, I'm glad you're okay. Lucky I was out when I was."

We both held on to the heavy silence that followed, thinking our own thoughts about what happened.

"Anyway," he said. "I'm Santos."

"Mercy."

"I know who you are." I must've given him a look because he sat back on his heels and gestured to the land behind us. "Mercy Farm. I'm your next-door neighbor. Been meaning to introduce myself but getting things up and running has taken a bit."

So. He was the man who bought Mr. Consuelo's place. He must have had a lot of money to afford that, plus all the improvements he put in. I'd only ever seen him around there. I mean, it didn't look like he had a family or anything, so I often wondered what one man was supposed to do with all that land, never mind that Mr. Consuelo did plenty with it himself.

"You farming?"

"Sort of. I grow herbs and medicinal plants and do wildcrafting."

He could tell I didn't know what he was talking about, so he explained that wildcrafting was when you got out and sustainably harvested stuff from nature.

I shrugged. "What do you do with all that, then?"

"I make soaps and balms. Medicine. Things like that. I use a lot of traditional recipes I learned from my mom. You should come by sometime, and I could show you around."

I raised my brows, and he must have guessed that I was thinking about how a bunch of soap could pay for all that land and the renovations he did before moving in because he added, "I work in tech but do this on the side."

"Like a hobby?" I had no idea why anyone would put in that kind of work for fun.

"Like a calling," he corrected. "I'm good with computers, and I'm good with plants. Somehow, they both brought me here. Can't do one or the other—I need both."

I nodded. If it was one thing I understood, it was the drive to plant things and make your home on a piece of land that spoke to you. Still, I couldn't quite wrap my head around why he'd need so much land for that.

"So...you're just, like, filling up those acres with a bunch of herbs?"

He laughed at that. "Some of it. I've got plans for the rest."

He didn't elaborate, and I could tell that the subject was closed, though I got the sense that he wouldn't do anything bad to the land. I couldn't tell you how I knew that, I just did. Mr. Consuelo was a good man, and the land wouldn't settle for anything less than a good man to replace him.

"What're those tattoos about?" I asked because, Lord help me, I couldn't stop looking at his muscled arms and really wanted to know.

He turned his wrists out to look at them. One was a pair of angel wings, the other was what looked like to be sprigs of lavender or rosemary.

"These? They're just something I got with some friends awhile back."

It wasn't the whole story, and we both knew it. There's no way a bunch of men would get together to get tattoos of herbs and angel wings, even if they were drunk. But I had plenty of secrets of my own, so who was I to judge? Still, that man was full of mysteries, and I wanted to know each and every one of them.

He insisted on walking me home. He held me by the elbow to make sure I didn't slip, and I tried not to think about what a sight I was covered head to

toe in mud. It made me feel strangely like one of
those girls in school who had their sweethearts walk
them home. I used to be so jealous of them. I mean,
I was terrified of ending up with the wrong man
and stuck in this stupid town for good, but I also
wanted to know what it felt like to be fussed over
and kissed.

Sherry and I used to watch them over our milk-
shakes at the diner and think about how nice it
would be to have someone wrap their jacket around
you and hold your hand and make sure you got
home safe. Of course, now I was coated in mud and
didn't look anything like those girls in their pretty
dresses. I'd never really worn one of them. That was
more Sherry's style.

We made it to my back porch—I didn't even
bother with the front door since it was easier to
peel off all my clothes by the laundry room in the
back. Anyway, he'd already seen me at my worst, so
what was the point of putting on airs and making
him take me to the front door? I whirled on him,
though, when we got to that back door. Nobody had
been on this land except me, my mom, Sherry, Mr.
Consuelo, and a kid named Miguel who helped me
out part-time in exchange for cash and produce.
Oh, and those little shits who used to vandalize my
house, but it had been years since that had happened.

Honestly? They only stopped because right before my house burned down, I got it in my head to
bury that tin can with my father's wallet in it right
at the front of my property, like I told you earlier. I
figured if it kept one bad man away, it would keep
the rest away, too. And I was right. Didn't do a damn
thing for La Llorona, though. She came and went

as she pleased, though I was trying my darnedest to get her to know her place, which wasn't on my land. All by way of saying, it was weird having someone new on my property. It was also weird knowing that he was a good man—he wouldn't have been able to set foot on it otherwise.

So, I told him, "Thanks for your help, I can take it from here," and walked through the back door, locked it behind me, stripped off my clothes, and marched up the stairs to my shower naked as the day I was born except for all that mud.

It took forever to get it off me, I mean, forever. I had to wash out my hair three times and soap myself down for so long, my skin was raw from the scrubbing. When I got out of the shower, it was ringed with mud, but I didn't have the energy to clean it just yet. Not after I'd just spent all that energy cleansing myself from her bitter spirit. Still, I knew it wasn't safe to leave a ring like that. La Llorona would take any foothold she could, so I wrapped my hair in a towel and wrapped myself in another one and got to work scrubbing my shower.

When all evidence of that morning's almost-baptism was gone, I opened the bathroom window wide to let in some fresh air. That was when I saw Santos. There he was, still on my porch, leaning against the railing casual as could be, as if I hadn't just taken half the morning cleaning myself up.

I hurried to my bedroom and threw on a t-shirt and clean pair of overalls, letting my long, half-dried hair hang loose behind me. I padded to the back door in my bare feet and swung it open.

"You still here?"

"Well, I left to get some ointment, but now I'm back." He held out a little blue jar.

"Why?"

He raised a brow, and I felt ashamed for my bad manners. Lord, I wasn't the best at this social stuff to begin with, but since Mr. Consuelo had left, I hadn't had much practice unless it was business-related.

"Figured you'd need some extra medicine after what you went through."

I knew he wouldn't go away until I used what was in that little jar of his, so I gave up and let him rub it on me.

It smelled good, like sunrise and citrus. And when he rubbed it across my scratched-up arms and even my shoulders, I felt the sweetest, deepest warmth seep into my bones, and I thought this must be what love feels like.

"Damn, those bushes sure got to you," he said, taking in the angry red claw marks across my limbs. I didn't bother to correct him, just murmured, and let him keep rubbing me all over like some kind of wild hedonist.

Of course, I felt stupid after and tried to forget that I hadn't been touched in a long time. Not that I knew much about touch, but Sherry and I hugged often. My mom would put her hand on my shoulder, right where La Llorona holds me now, when she knew I was getting flighty and too full of dreams, and I needed to be grounded. Once in a while, Mr. Consuelo would put a hand on my shoulder, too, which was the closest he came to a hug, probably so as not to scare me, skittish as I was about men in general. But that was about it.

So, you can understand how touch-starved I was after all those years. Don't ask me how many—I already told you I was on the wrong side of thirty and that's more than I was willing to divulge to begin with. It's none of your business, and I wish you and this whole stupid town would stop fixating on my age and marital status.

Anyway, Santos rubbed his ointment all up and down my arms and across my shoulders, even my legs when he talked me into rolling up my overalls. For a few minutes, I was in heaven.

It was like sunshine. When he rubbed it along her handprint scar on my shoulder, for the first time in ages, I felt desert heat instead of cold muddy water in my soul. It was such a sharp, sweet feeling that I flinched.

"Mercy." The way he said my name sounded like a prayer. Not the kind of church prayer that makes you hate yourself. The way it passed his lips was like a revelation. I'd never heard my name sound so beautiful. I blushed hard and deep all the way down to my toes.

"Mercy, you okay?"

I got back to myself. "Yeah," I said. "It's just a little sore is all." I pulled my overall strap over my shoulder and turned to face him.

"What's in that anyway?"

"Calendula. Beeswax. Juniper. Bunch of other stuff. Ingredients are on the back."

He handed me the jar, and for the rest of the week when I applied that salve to my body, I thought of his hands on me.

It wasn't a bad birthday as far as birthdays went.

◆

After a while, it got so that I needed help around the farm from time to time. I did what Mr. Consuelo suggested and waited until the right person came along to help me. I didn't want to advertise because I didn't want to stir up all those goons who used to vandalize the property, so I put it about to a few trustworthy people that I might be interested in some help if the person was the right fit.

That was how I met Miguel. He was the young kid I told you about who came around one day and asked if there was any work needing to be done. He was so polite and so earnest—that's one of the words I learned from those library books—that I let him chop wood and pick weeds a few times a week in exchange for produce and, sometimes, cash. He had a good feeling to him and, of course, he easily walked on the property past the buried can with my father's wallet wrapped in chicken wire, so I knew he was okay right from the get-go.

He was sort of goofy-looking, if I'm being honest. And if I'm being really honest, he reminded me of myself when I was that young. He was all knees and elbows just like I was, as if he weren't quite comfortable in his own skin. He also had this perpetually dreamy look on his face, like he could see potential in things nobody else could. He had the tan skin of a kid who could never pass as white and the dark brown eyes and muddy hair to match. He was the same height as me, too, though I was sturdier, even if that's not a word that should be applied to a woman. You don't make a living as a farmer, even a small one like myself, without developing a few muscles.

I always saw him around town with a book stuffed in his back pocket or open in front of his face. I figured if he liked reading so much, he must be decent. Plus, I'd seen him a time or two with his mom, and when no one was looking, he was really nice to her. I mean, he was nice to her when people were looking, too, but it's what a person does when people aren't looking that really matters.

When I found out he was working for me to keep food on his mother's table—she had a string of deadbeats in and out of her door that were good for nothing but trouble and heartache—it occurred to me that it wasn't just us women that were trying to sort through the things that got passed down to us. Between him and Santos, I was beginning to see there were men out there doing their best to figure out a better way of going about life.

So, we struck up a bit of a friendship, Miguel and me. He worked his way up to steady part-time work at the farm, and it went a long way to ease my workload, especially with the weeds, which never seemed to go away no matter how much you told them they weren't welcome. We talked about books, and eventually, it came out that he was hoping to do something someday. Maybe write a book or travel the world or both. All those big, bold thoughts—and believe me, he had a lot of them—took me back to when I was his age, thinking about city life and big houses. There was something to be said about being that young and hopeful. It was refreshing but made me sad, too, and I cried quietly into one of my mason jars until the feeling went away.

One time, I caught him staring at me. Not like a pervert, mind you. But in the kind of way a person looks at you when they're wondering. Like the way I looked at Sherry's aunt what feels like a lifetime ago. I just hope what he saw was worth the looking.

◆

Next time I talked to Santos, I was digging up dead flowers along the wooden fence that separated our property. I'd seen him around, sure. It was hard not to, seeing as Mr. Consuelo's house was so close to my property, but we hadn't really talked since the river incident. Not for the first time, I wondered what a single man was going to do with all that land. I mean, there was too much of it for just herbs. Anyway, it wasn't really my business.

That was what La Llorona was telling me when she gave the hollyhocks root rot that grew along the fence that separated our properties. She pushed water up from the river and used it to eat away at their roots like she was trying to do to mine. There was no saving hollyhocks once that fungus got on them. I was pulling them out and treating the soil so I could grow more.

Don't think I didn't understand her subtext either. She just wanted me to know that it was only a matter of time before I succumbed to the rotten thing she was. Me? I thought it was mighty rich that she compared herself to a fungus and me to a fearless flower and even tried to make myself laugh about it.

But I also knew I wouldn't be laughing come nightfall.

Daylight made me brave, but there was a real part of me that worried she had infected me beyond repair, and that I was slowly fading like those hollyhocks pressed up at the edge of the fence between my farm and Mr. Consuelo's—Santos's—property. Fading like my mother did. It would start with yellowing leaves, then flower buds that wouldn't quite open, then the stems would cave in on themselves, and the flowers that could survive anything with a little water and a lot of sunlight would be gone just like that. I told myself I didn't have time for that kind of thinking, but I knew I could only suppress that line of thought for so long. The fears were stronger in the moonlight.

I also couldn't ignore the fact that she left the hollyhocks in my front yard intact. It was...significant that she attacked the ones between me and Santos. I knew she wasn't at all happy that he rescued me, but it was more than that. Like she didn't like the way I liked him so much. And Lord help me, I did. Or maybe I just wanted more of that salve he'd made. At any rate, when I saw him walking across his field toward me carrying a small basket, I thought of his warm hands on my shoulders, and then I thought of the chickens she'd ripped up a few years back, and my heart got tight.

"Hoping I'd run into you again."

He leaned against the short coyote fence, looking more handsome than any man had a right to. He had this gentle way about him, even though he looked a little rough with the broken nose and a few light scars running across his knuckles. Then there I was, once again muddy in my overalls, looking like I'd fought a puddle and lost.

"Seems only likely, since we're neighbors." I kept digging up the dead hollyhocks and tossing them in a pile behind me.

"How're you doing?"

"What's it to you?" Dig. Dig. Dig.

"Just wanted to make sure you were doing okay after what happened by the river last week."

"I'm fine."

"Okay, then. I can see you're busy, so I'll get out of your hair."

I finally dared to glance up at him, and I couldn't take what I saw there. He looked mildly offended. Now I'm not a cruel person by nature, despite what the town says, and I didn't have it in me to be rude. He didn't deserve my coldness, even if I was trying to protect him. I'd just have to figure out another way to keep her away from him.

I rested my foot on the shovel and let out a long sigh. "Sorry. It's just been a rough week."

"Maybe these'll help." His features relaxed and he propped up the basket on the fence between us. Behind him, the sun was a pink stain above the mountains.

"What's all this?"

"Thought you might like to try some of my bubble bath. It's got hops and valerian root in there to help you relax, plus roses for the scent."

As if I needed to relax!

"I don't do bubble baths," I told him.

"I thought all women liked bubble baths."

"Not me," I said and handed the basket back again, tasting soapy bubbles at the back of my throat, feeling them pile up in my lungs.

"Okay then, how about soap? You like soap?"

"Sure. I mean, I use it."

"Well then, take my lemon balm soap." He reached into the basket and handed me two bars.

They smelled like the first day of spring. I was too weak to reject them, so I said thanks and told him that I liked that ointment he'd made, too.

"All right, then, I'll make sure to bring you some next time."

I didn't want him to think I was greedy, and I also didn't want to owe him anything. I couldn't figure out why he was being so nice.

"You don't have to. I just meant to say thanks is all."

"It's no problem. I'm happy to share."

Like I said, I was weak and really did want more of that salve, but I didn't want handouts.

"Well, okay, I'll take some, but only if you take some of my turnips, or whatever else you might like."

"It's a deal," he said and reached across the fence to shake my hand.

I may have held on a touch too long. I was a woman after all, not a saint, and I couldn't help enjoying the feel of my hand in his.

"Sorry about your hollyhocks," he said. We both gazed at the yellowed stalks behind me, and I felt sad all over again.

"What do you know about curses?" I asked him before I could think better of it.

He said he didn't deal in curses, only medicine.

"Wish I knew what that felt like."

"Seems to me you do."

"What's that supposed to mean?"

He gestured to the land behind me with his chin. I looked out across the freshly turned and seeded field and for the first time saw my plot of land the way outsiders might see it. Fertile earth in the middle of a desert land.

"Enjoy your soap," he said and walked on back to his house.

That night, I used his soap, and it was the first time in a shower I didn't feel the shadow of La

Llorona hovering over me or worry about root rot metaphors.

♦

I read this book where the heroine liked to pour herself a glass of wine at night and sit in front of the fire and read a book. And I read another one where the woman loved her house slippers. Around that time, the farm was doing well. Santos had even mentioned helping me put up a website and maybe getting a social media presence, though I didn't know what I'd do with all that.

Santos said his whole business was online, which freed up a lot of time, since it meant he didn't have to do the market and festival scenes or depend on storefronts to move his goods. It gave him more time to work on his other project: turning his land into a community garden and educational center of sorts where people could learn the fundamentals of sustainable agriculture. I liked the idea and wished there had been a place like that for me when I was growing up. Though come to think of it, there had been—Mr. Consuelo's farm. Santos had so many ideas, it made my head spin, but it was also kind of wonderful to listen to someone who knew how to dream big then make it happen.

I hadn't taken him up on that offer yet—wasn't sure I would—but it did get me thinking about easier ways of doing things, so I had more time to enjoy all I'd worked for. He'd explained to me one time what he meant when he called what we did medicine, and why he always made my name sound like a delicious prayer, if ever there was such a thing.

"I've always liked the name Mercy—had a lot of good luck with it." He smiled a little wolfishly then but wouldn't expand on it. Somehow, I didn't think he was talking about other women. At least, I hoped not.

I leaned against my truck, the bed half full of empty crates. The Esperanza Growers' Market had wiped me out again, literally and figuratively, but I wasn't about to complain about the bundle of cash I'd made. It wasn't too long ago when I only dreamed about making that kind of money. Still, I was bone-tired, and he looked fresh as could be in a black t-shirt, leather jacket, jeans, and biker boots.

"You going out tonight?" He sure looked ready for a night on the town, and once again, I tried to curb the pangs of jealousy that ripped through me.

"Just for a cruise," he said.

He rested a hand on the seat of this gorgeous bike, one of those classic old motorcycles. I couldn't help imagining myself riding on it, with my arms wrapped around his waist as we cruised up and down the highway that separated us from the Shadow Lands.

"What about you?"

I shrugged, trying to act casual, like going out on a Saturday night was a regular thing, even though I never in my life had done that. "Think I'll stay in tonight. Feel like lying low."

Of course, by that, I meant flop into bed as soon as I could. Anyway, I didn't want him knowing that.

"You don't like dancing? I'm sure the men'd be lining up to dance with you."

I shrugged again, aiming for casual, though my stomach was equal parts butterflies that he thought

I was desirable and panic at the thought of men wanting me.

"It's been a long day," I explained, then quickly changed the subject. "Santos, what did you mean when you said I dealt in medicine?"

He looked surprised by that. "I thought you knew."

I gave him a blank stare.

"It's like healing but for the spirit, not just the body."

So, it was a Native thing, like the stuff my mother did but never talked about. Santos probably thought I knew something about it because of the way I looked—I tried not to be too pleased that he could tell I wasn't white—but that was a buried legacy.

Santos rode off into the sunset—literally, I didn't make that up—while I went about unloading. He said he'd like to help, but he had a meeting he had to make, and honestly, I was glad because he'd given me a lot to think about. Like the whole reason I was doing what I was doing was to make things better for myself and those that came after me.

I started to think maybe it was okay to have things around the house that made me happy. So, I bought these outrageous fur-lined purple slippers that were on sale at some outdoor market the next time I went into the city and started wearing them around the house. I bought a bundle of books, too, and let myself enjoy them. These beat-up old things with outrageous covers and even more outrageous plots. I was coming to enjoy outrageous things, as it turned out. I didn't even throw them out when I was done with them. Instead, I stacked them on my nightstand until one day I had so many, I bought myself a whole bookshelf to house them.

It was nice having them around. Nice not denying myself the enjoyment of those stories and those slippers.

♦

The next night, I was lured outside by the sound of soft music floating over my field. It was a cool spring evening, and the music danced over to my side of the fence with the soft breeze while I was out checking my plants. I could make out Santos sitting on his porch with an old record player, a stack of records, and a beer at his side. He played boleros and classic cantos—soft, heady music that made me think of two-story homes and big vases full of flowers.

I followed that noise to the fence between us, rested my forearms against it, and closed my eyes and swayed to the luscious melodies. They reminded me of my mother—she only ever sang the love songs. When I opened my eyes, he was in front of me, and I got self-conscious and stood up straight.

"Would you like to dance?" he asked.

My body went all rigid, and I looked at him sharply, like he was trying to pull something over on me. I should have known he'd want something for those nice soaps he'd given me.

He must have read something in my face because he just laughed in that soft, warm way of his and said I didn't have to dance if I didn't want to. I turned beet red and marched back to my house and bolted the door. That night and for each night after, he cranked up that record player of his so that I could hear that intoxicating music from inside my home.

That gave me a lot to think about.

♦

So, I got older day by day, and life was pretty good, all things considered. I still got lonely, but I figured as long as La Llorona howled and raged at me every night, living alone was for the best. She was like a wound that wouldn't heal, but I managed all the same, and slowly but surely, things started growing around her.

I still left Sherry harvest baskets and was getting to the point where I had to figure out what to do with all the mason jars full of tears piling up in my pantry. Business was good, too. I kept my farm small and profitable, focused only on the things I could grow really well—all those root veggies, corn, beans, and squash, plus a few herbs and greens.

I got into canning, too, so I could have another income stream come the leaner months and something to keep me busy when the days were short and the nights seemed to go on forever. Between that and my beeswax candles, I was doing all right. Those I made just because I liked them and the way they made my home smell, but they also brought in a pretty penny at the market. Plus, they were a nice way to fill my time when La Llorona wanted me to feel how long and dark winter could be. They filled my home with a honeyed scent and reminded me of my mother so much, it was like I could feel her in the kitchen with me sometimes.

I liked having all my bases covered, especially considering we were headed for another drought. I'd already managed to survive two when other newer farms around the area had folded. Between that and La Llorona generally trying to get me to hate myself and my life, well, I had a lot on my mind most days.

I was picking squash bugs off the plant blossoms early one morning—best to get that done when those critters are active—and hating La Llorona something fierce. Okay, I knew squash bugs were pretty common, so I wasn't blaming them on that water witch, but I was blaming her for a terrible night's sleep. She spent the whole dang night weeping and wailing and rattling my windows louder than usual, which kept me tossing and turning. I woke up late and went straight to work, feeling like nothing would make me feel better except time on the land. There's a bone-deep satisfaction that comes from picking off those little bugs and squashing them with your gloved hands. I imagined each one was La Llorona and crushed them with a vicious glee.

If only it were that easy to get rid of her.

I was just about done when I saw Santos walking across my field with a small tote bag across his shoulder. I could almost smell the rosemary, lavender, and lemon balm planted in his fields as the breeze brought him closer to me. I'd wondered about him more than once, especially since he hadn't yet taken me up on my offer of produce. He spent his days between his work in tech, whatever that meant, planting, and getting that educational side of things going. When he wasn't doing all that, he was making his soaps and lotions and things in Mr. Consuelo's old barn, which had been outfitted into a kitchen-type area. He kept busy, but he never seemed to be in a rush.

Like now.

There he was, probably with as much work to do as me or more, but he strolled over to the fence and called out, "Thought you might like some breakfast!"

I took off my gloves, now covered in squash bug guts, and headed over.

"Here I thought you were after my vegetables," I said, trying for a joke and apparently succeeding, by the way he laughed as he pulled out a thermos and two bundles wrapped in foil. Guess he was serious about that breakfast.

"I'll take anything you want to give me, Mercy."

The way he said it made me pause and pull inside myself and blush to my core all at the same time. He must have guessed that the comment had put me off, because he held up one of the foiled objects.

"Breakfast burrito?"

"You know what they say about me, right?" I had to know. He was so nice, so generous with himself, I had to know if he knew the real me.

"I've heard there are no better vegetables than those that come from Mercy Farm."

"No, I mean the names they call me."

"Sure, I've heard them." He scratched his chin where some stubble was trying to grow itself into a beard. "My favorite's—"

"Don't tell me." I didn't want to hear them from his lips—those lips that made my name sound so beautiful. Whore. Shrew. Witch. Spinster. Slut. Those were the words that kept me up at night when La Llorona was too tired to bother with me.

"What's got you so tied up in knots?" He reached out and pulled my loose overall strap back up over my shoulder.

"Why are you so nice to me?"

That got him. He ran his fingers through his long black hair and toed the ground with his boots—the only things he wore that ever seemed muddy. "Well, Mercy, isn't it obvious?"

"No, not to me."

Then he gave me this look, like he pitied me, but it was gone before I could think to feel ashamed. "Because I like you."

I believed him, too. I mean, why else would he always be hanging around the fence that divided our properties trying to talk to me? Or playing his records for me at night? His farm was bigger than mine, which meant he had more money than me, especially with all he was planning to do with it, so he wasn't after my land or my water rights—he had his own. He never tried any funny business either, which meant he wasn't a creep. So, I took the burrito he offered and let him pour me a cup of coffee from that big thermos of his.

I tell you, I have never had a breakfast burrito taste so delicious. Freshly scrambled eggs, green chile, beans, and cheese all wrapped in a soft flour tortilla. Simple but heavenly.

"You make this?" I asked around a mouthful of that rolled-up perfection.

"Yup."

I groaned in response like the weak woman that I was, and together we polished off the rest of our burritos in companionable silence. After, I invited him over to my field to pick some beets, turnips, and radishes for all the nice soaps and salves he'd given me. I loaded them into one of my Mercy Farm totes, though he said I didn't need to bother with a bag, but I insisted.

"You tell me when you want more and just bring the bag over, and I'll fill it up," I said.

Breakfast and his kindness had made me bold. I certainly was in a much better mood than when I'd woken up. The sleepless night felt like a lifetime ago.

"Okay, thanks," he said, shouldering his bags and heading to his side of the fence. He turned back halfway and shouted, "Miracle Mercy!"

"What?" I wasn't sure I'd heard him right.

"That's what they call you." He smiled. "Miracle Mercy."

So, like I said, La Llorona liked to leave little presents for me. But so did Santos. Him and me got in the habit of sharing our goods. He gave me his fine soaps and lotions, and I gave him turnips and beeswax candles. After a bit, we struck up a solid friendship. After all these years, I never thought I'd be friends with a man, let alone two. Three, if you counted Mr. Consuelo, which I did because I still smiled every time he sent me a postcard.

All in all, it wasn't a half-bad life I'd built for myself. In fact, it was shaping up to be pretty darn nice. At night, when I was alone in bed and couldn't sleep, I kept going back to what Santos said they called me around town now. Course, there were those that still said bad things about me, but not as much. Not like it was when I was younger.

He said it was because of all I'd survived, and I was surprised that he knew so much about me. I tried not to feel too pleased when he confessed he'd asked around about me. I tried even harder not to care that the stories that they told about me had changed. I was no longer the witch. I was the miracle woman, the one who'd survived a father who abandoned her (course, they didn't know the whole story), her mother's premature death, a burned-down house, and two severe droughts. Somehow, I'd managed to come out the other side not just alive but thriving.

The way he said my name—Miracle Mercy—like it was a fact. Well, that got me thinking some more.

I was feeling fine one night, enjoying the luxury of those books and my slippers. I'd taken to savoring a glass of wine after dinner and curling up on the sofa and reading just like that heroine in that one book. Sometimes, I even lit beeswax candles when it was too warm for a fire.

The wine came from a local vineyard across the way. The owners contacted me a while back to see about getting some of my produce for this farm-to-table restaurant they were opening. They were a nice husband-and-wife team who dressed in old-timey clothes—that's the only term I could think to describe her pioneer dress and his suspenders—and wanted to invest in their own vineyard after running several in Napa Valley.

They invited me over and had me sample their products and explained how they were going to repurpose an old barn on the vineyard to make a rustic pop-up restaurant that featured local goods. They served me some wine and these small pieces of tasty bread that were slathered in goat cheese, topped with beets, and what they called micro-greens, which was just really a bunch of sprouts before the plants really got going, and it wasn't half bad. I didn't know much about wine, but I thought theirs tasted good.

I didn't understand much of what they said either, any more than I could see why someone would want to have a handlebar mustache, but who was I to judge? Seemed like they used a lot of fancy words for some pretty basic concepts, like the fact that they cared about organic, sustainable, and eq-uitable practices, but they were so proud of them-selves for what they knew, so I let them enjoy their thoughts. Anyway, I liked the idea of taking something abandoned and broken and making it beautiful again, and how they insisted on paying what a person's labor was worth, especially when I saw the big fat number they were willing to offer for the sake of my produce. I liked anything that made sound business sense. So, we struck up a deal, which included a case of their wine every so often.

Mercy Farm was doing well, and this thing with the vineyard would help me turn more of a profit sooner rather than later, which was why I was feel-ing mighty proud of myself and the life I'd built from the ashes of my old home. I didn't have much, but everything I did have was nice and well cared for. I couldn't tolerate messes and broken things, not like what I grew up with. I was even decorating a bit with simple art, Navajo rugs, and other things I collected from the markets I went to.

That night, Santos was playing his records like he usually did, and I was curled up on the couch, lis-tening to their honeyed melodies. I held a racy paperback in my hand but didn't read it much. Instead, I sipped my wine and took in my living room, which was clean and homey, and my slippers, which were ridiculous and beautiful and not something a farmer should really have. All of a sudden, I got this warm, full feeling inside my chest, like sunlight or the way you feel after digging up a mighty fine bunch of carrots. I smiled, thinking of Santos turning up the volume for me, and even though we were in our separate homes, there was a cozy companionship between us each night as we shared in this ritual.

Of course, this was when she would try to ruin things for me.

I felt so good, so fine, that it took me a minute to realize why my heart got tight and that warm luscious feeling all over my body vanished like early morning mist when the sun came up. That song. The one about her and all the grief she suffered, and all the sorrow she made us carry because she did not want to weep alone.

My mind went to the pantry full of mason jars, and I got right mad. I hopped up from the couch and went out my back door, across my plant rows, over the coyote fence, past the cottonwood that used to hold me close, and right up to Santos's house. The light was fading and already a sliver of moon was out.

He was there, like he always was, on that old rocking chair, with the record player sitting on a wooden table and the records leaning against it. He held a mug of tea and was going to put it to his lips when I marched right up to him and told him to turn that damned thing off right now.

Around that time, I came to my senses, and had two feelings running through me. One was fear. You never confronted a man like that without getting the back end of his hand. The second was shame. It wasn't his fault that she had intruded on our nightly ritual or that I grew up expecting the worst from a man.

I took a deep breath and said, "I just hate that song, is all."

He smiled that slow smile of his and lifted the needle off the record player. The silence was sweet, swallowed up only by the summer crickets and cicadas.

"Okay," he said. "So, what songs do you like?"

I saw him take in my purple slippers, my long wild hair, and my pajamas that had little strawberries all over them, and I suddenly felt foolish and naked. But he wasn't laughing at me, and he wasn't angry at my outburst. I crossed my arms over my chest and considered it.

"I like the song about the wild desert rose."

I didn't know what else to say, so I turned right back around and didn't stop walking until I was back in my own kitchen, door bolted behind me.

He played that song for me every night after that. The first song to start the evening and the last song to close out the night.

That gave me even more to think about.

♦

The more time that passed, the more I got to thinking about what Santos said about Mercy Farm being medicine, and the more I liked the idea of being Miracle Mercy. I mean, it felt like a big name to grow into, but what else was there to do?

The woman two farms down from me, who sings those bitter cantos, could eat my food and know the grace of joy pass her lips. Her songs would be like those of the birds who made their home in the Bosque. The young girls in the town would begin to expect more and want more than just endurance, and their mothers would learn not to pass their sorrows on.

And the men...they would eat this medicine, and there would be more Miguels, and Santoses, and Mr. Consuelos. There would be more women like my mother, too, and more girls like Sherry, only they wouldn't throw away their future because they were afraid of a life without limits. Or maybe it would just weaken La Llorona's hold enough to give them a fighting chance. More souls like Sherry's aunt, who make their own life for themselves on their own terms.

I saw her once, you know, at the Esperanza Growers' Market. She was three stalls down buying some radishes, and I wanted to tell her mine were better and that I'd give them to her for free. She had filled out some since I'd last seen her and there was gray in her hair. That man of hers had a girl on his shoulders and she had her arm around the shoulders of another girl that looked just shy of puberty. They looked happy, and there was a moment—just one quick second—when her eyes caught mine, and I knew she knew who I was. I also knew she would never come by my stall and try my medicine. Sometimes the only way out is a clean break, and I didn't hold it against her one bit. It's what I would have done, given the chance. Anyway, that's not how things went for me, but I was happy for her, and I got to thinking a lot about what was the whole point of what happened to me.

If I was Miracle Mercy, then I could heal things. People. Like Sherry. I'd seen her around town a few times in the past month and noticed there was a little color back in her cheeks and the hemline of her dress was a little shorter. The more I thought about it, the more it felt like a real possibility that I could bring her back from that riverbed. Maybe, just maybe, being Miracle Mercy could speed up the process that watered down the hold La Llorona had on the women in our family. Maybe it wouldn't take generations to break the bonds of baptism this time. Maybe, in a few years, Sherry would be back to herself.

Now don't think I was getting carried away. I knew there was only so much one little turnip could do, even if I was developing a reputation for growing some great varietals like red and purple turnips. Let's just say that those who wanted my medicine—and yeah, Santos had gotten me think-ing about what I was doing, the business of grow-ing things, as medicine—they'd find it. Just like I latched on to Sherry's aunt's life and used it as a template for my own. I couldn't make people take my medicine, but it was there if they wanted it.

I wanted to break the spell she had us under.

Santos had to leave town for a week. He seemed restless when he told me he was heading up to Esperanza for a bit, and there was a hard look to his face when he mounted his motorcycle and took off. He'd asked me to keep an eye on things for him, and I promised I would. Santos didn't say why he had to leave or what he had to do, and I didn't ask. He didn't pry into my life, and I extended the same courtesy.

I missed him something fierce, though, and the nights felt dark and lonely without his records to serenade me. The days were long and hard, the summer heat taking it out of me, and I had to struggle not to be in a mood. I pretended not to notice when seven days had passed, and that he would be back to his farm that very morning if he was a man of his word.

He was.

I found him leaning against his side of the coyote fence, more relaxed than the last time I'd seen him, and looking fresh with hair still wet from the shower and a Mercy Farm t-shirt on. I strolled up to him, casual as could be, in my overalls and work boots. I may or may not have worn new overalls and tried to tame my wild black hair into a braid. I stopped short, though, when I saw what he held in his hands. Wild desert roses. Fat bold blooms the color of romance and deep blushes with petals that spread themselves wide open for the morning light. These weren't the tight, hard buds of hothouse roses, but wanton luscious flowers that grew even in the hardest desert conditions with a little sunshine and a little praise. That warm, glowing feeling raced through my body again and was quickly chased away by panic.

"What're those about?" I asked without preamble. "They for your lady?"

"Don't have one of those. Yet." He didn't smile this time, but his eyes were smokey and, well, intimate, and I didn't know what to think about that. I tried not to look at his strong arms or the tattoos on his wrists that I was dying to touch.

"How was the city?" Yeah, I was a coward and changed the subject soon as I could.

He shrugged. "City's the city."

"Please! There's so much to do up there. You telling me you didn't have any fun?"

He shrugged again and held out the roses to me. "Spent the whole time thinking about desert roses."

I took them like the sucker that I was and inhaled their sweet perfume. Then I came to my senses and gave him a good hard look.

"Be real with me, Santos. You flirting with me?"

Now this really got him. He laughed, and it was a good, full minute before he could get a sentence out. "Mercy."

There he went again, making my name sound like something to be proud of. "Mercy, don't you know I've been flirting with you this whole time? I know I'm out of practice, but I can't be that bad."

Not bad at all, I thought, though I had little enough experience with flirting.

But what I said was, "Don't you know I'm old?"

He knew my age, too, because he'd wheedled it out of me once, despite my best efforts. I even let it slip that I didn't do birthdays, and he said we'd have to change that, and maybe I'd let him. Still wasn't budging on the bubble bath thing, though.

He laughed again, harder and longer this time.

"Mercy"—I was getting addicted to the way he said my name—"how can you be old when you're as old as me, and I don't think I'm old at all?"

That was the kind of logic I wasn't prepared for.

"It's different for women," I explained. "I mean, that's how it is between men and women."

"Well, maybe it shouldn't be."

I didn't have an answer for that, so I kept his flowers and gave him one last look over my shoulder before heading back to the house.

Lord! That man filled my head with thoughts.

I thought about the years I'd spent being called a spinster, and how I was, and how age was just a number. Don't ask me how old I was by then—that's none of your business and that's not the point. The point is, well, I don't remember, so I guess I'll just move on to the next bit here.

So, there I was, with this gorgeous—and I mean gorgeous—bouquet of desert roses, walking back to my adobe home, when I stopped and finally saw things as they were. The way Santos saw me and maybe even how Miguel saw me. And I tell you, I laughed so hard and so long, I almost cried. The only thing that kept me from spilling tears was the fact that I was low on mason jars and had to be careful.

There it was right in front of me.

I couldn't believe it took me so long to see it. A two-story house. A nice one, too. With a staircase. Never mind there weren't two—this was not the time to quibble over details. And a fat bouquet of red roses to put in my entryway. Well, I'll be. It'd been a while since I'd thought of that dream, and here I'd been building it all this time.

I couldn't wait to tell Sherry about this and that thought sobered me. In fact, it made me so sorrowful, the tears started spilling from my eyes, and I had to run into the house for the last of the mason jars before something bad happened.

◆

The next day, I saw I did spill some tears on some dry, cracked earth next to my porch. Just one, really. There was a big fat turnip where my tears had been, and I pulled it out of the ground, dusted it off, and took a bite. What else was I supposed to do? It tasted sharp and a little sweet, like sweat or tears but in a good way. Then I went inside and locked the door and waited all day for something bad to happen.

But nothing did.

I finally got up when my bones were achy from sitting all day, and I didn't have the strength to be still anymore. I opened my front door wide and looked at the rich farmland spread before me in the fading light. La Llorona was quiet that night.

Maybe Mercy Farm was medicine after all.

◆

I was coming to learn that La Llorona's power was a two-way street.

I'd done my fair share of crying over the years. I had more sorrows than a woman could keep track of. When I couldn't hold it in any longer, and the pain overtook me like a heavy monsoon rain, I poured all that sorrow into my mason jars and kept them in my pantry for safekeeping.

I knew what it was to feel bone-deep loneliness. I knew what it was to have to carry a pocketknife in case any of the men in town got any ideas when they saw me walking alone. I knew what it was to be feared and reviled by people I'd never even met. I knew what it meant to be marked by that water witch, so much so my very tears were a danger. And I knew what it was to use those tears to wish someone gone. But lately, I'd been wondering if I couldn't use them for other things. If all that sorrow could take away life, couldn't it give life, too?

I couldn't get that tear-soaked turnip out of my head. I mean, here I was, a grown woman, and I thought about turnips more than a body ought to. But they'd done right by me before, so it stood to reason that I should listen to what they had to say now.

Here's what they told me: La Llorona could feel me as much as I felt her. She raged and scraped angry tree branches across my windows, so I shrank under my covers at night, afraid of the dark. I lit beeswax candles and filled my front yard and fence line with hollyhocks, so she sank to the bottom of the river come morning, afraid of the light. It was an old road we walked together, day after day, night after night, and the more we walked this path, the more I learned about her.

I'd been doing a lot of thinking, thinking about what Santos said about my farm being medicine and about how some people—the right kind of people, according to him, more people than I could wrap my head around—called me Miracle Mercy.

See, I'd figured out a thing or two. Thinking about how she let go of me that night on the riverbank all those years ago—and she did, sure as I was that Sherry had. Well, I'm not actually sure about that with Sherry, but sometimes I wonder. Maybe it was the way I thought about the things that made me happy, or maybe it was Sherry giving me one last chance to get away. Or maybe it was because, underneath all my fear, I had enough strength to call out to the land and know that I wasn't alone, even though Sherry had given up. In any case, I was beginning to see that the thing the river witch feared most was life, and I didn't plan on wasting any more of mine, try as she might to get me to curl up inside myself and give up on the whole idea of the thing.

◆

After the last turnip and tears incident, I found myself grocery shopping in town for the stuff I couldn't grow or make myself. I was making my way to the checkout when I noticed three people whispering about me. It was strange because I realized people hadn't been whispering about me for some time, at least not where I could see them. For that matter, I couldn't remember the last time kids tried to throw stones at my windows or dare one another to knock on my door, not that they'd get far with my tin can ward and all.

But there they were—two men wearing the clothes that were supposed to look casual but I knew cost more than I made in a month—talking to one of the cashiers who never had a kind thing to say to me for as long as I knew him. One man looked older with salt-and-pepper hair cropped close and a warm, tanned skin, while the younger one was paler and dressed like a lumberjack. I didn't recognize them, but I knew that didn't mean anything.

People loved to gossip, and if they couldn't find drama, they'd make some.

I turned my cart into the checkout next to them, determined to go about my business and ignore their gazes. It was as I was loading up the last of my bagged groceries that they approached me. The older one introduced himself as José Rodriguez and his partner as Winston Brook. As we got to talking, it occurred to me that he didn't just mean business partner. I mean, I never put my arm around the waist of anyone I ever did business with. It got me thinking about how love looks a lot of different ways, and I was glad they decided to put down roots here. Enough people were leaving this town, and enough people were moving in to shake things up enough to make a real difference, such as it was. Even the church at the center of Main Street was looking rundown due to poor attendance and lack of donations and, boy, was that a beautiful thing to see!

Anyway, back to the matter at hand. José said he and Winston just bought the store. This rundown place that was older than sin and didn't have much in the way of goods. They wanted to spruce things up a bit. I tried not to look around at the faded tile and the walls desperately in need of a paint job, not to mention the shelving aisle that sagged in the middle and had been doing so since I was young. But the more they got to talking, the more I understood that "spruce things up" meant completely renovate and reinvent the place.

They wanted to make it a place where locals could get their basic needs met, but also the sort of spot tourists would come to on their way to the vineyard or the B&B that had opened up next to it a few years back. Their whole plan was to include as much local produce and crafts as possible to showcase the talent and beauty of the surrounding area.

Naturally, they thought of me and my turnips. Yeah, I know, I was getting a big head about my ability with seeds, but I had years of positive reinforcement on that end, so I figured it was okay. I liked them and what they were trying to do for the town, so I invited them down to my farm to sample some produce and take a look around. And they had one thing right, for all I originally resisted staying in Sueño: It was beautiful land. Big blue skies and a desert landscape that would have gone on forever, if it weren't for the mountains stopping them in the distance and the Rio Grande cutting through it and peppering it with cottonwoods.

So, we shook on it, and I went home feeling like I didn't even know my own town anymore. Which, considering what I used to know about it, was a good thing.

Still, with all that, I had a time of it keeping my spirits up. Take one blazing summer afternoon. It was too hot to be outdoors at certain times, so all my farm work had to be done in the early morning and late evenings. That meant midday was for house stuff, bills, and paperwork. I was cleaning up a pile of broken robin's eggs outside my kitchen door and thinking some pretty ugly thoughts about La Llorona. She liked to remind me about that year with the chickens any time she could. I kept wondering if I could use my tears to wish her dead, but I didn't think it would work, seeing as she'd been dead a long time and that hadn't made her go away for anybody.

I heard his footsteps before I saw him. Santos had taken to popping by regularly since last year when he'd moved in, though I never invited him in or even offered him a cup of coffee on the porch. We'd chat for a bit, and sometimes I'd give him produce, then he'd be on his way. He kept inviting me over to see what he'd done with Mr. Consuelo's farm, but I hadn't worked up the courage to take him up on it yet. Sometimes I felt like maybe there could be something between us, but every time I thought of crossing that fence again, images of slaughtered chickens and dead hollyhocks invaded my head and panic surged through me.

I set my broom down and quickly closed my kitchen door. I'd been cleaning out my kitchen, and all those mason jars filled with tears were piled on the table and the floor. I'd been trying to figure out where to put them all, now that there wasn't enough room in the pantry anymore. The thing is, I didn't want Santos to see them. I'll admit it: I was ashamed of them. The way he saw me was something beautiful, and I was worried that if he knew the kind of monster she'd made me into, he wouldn't come around anymore.

"That where you keep the dead bodies?"

I practically jumped out of my overalls and whirled around. I didn't realize he'd been so close. He was looking handsomer than any man had a right to, as usual. He had a Mercy Farm tote dangling from one hand and his other hand stuck in the back pocket of his jeans. His black hair was loose

around his shoulders—he never bothered with ty-
ing it back. I liked that about him, though I couldn't
say why. Same goes for his broken nose. Maybe
it was because he didn't look like the clean-cut
church boys I grew up with.

He was rough around the edges but all tender-
ness, too, like his tattoos that seemed like they belonged on a woman and not a man. I might have
watched him tending his plants a time or two when
I thought he wasn't looking. A man with hands as
big and loving as him had to be nothing but tender-
ness—the plants wouldn't take to him otherwise.
He told me once he used to ride his bike all over
the state, and I wondered if he was ever part of the
biker gang that patrolled the long strip of highway
between the Shadow Lands and the rest of rural
New Mexico. But he didn't talk much about his past,
and it wasn't my place to pry.

Didn't stop me from wondering, though.

"Dead bodies?" I tried to act casual and went back
to holding my broom.

"Yeah, that's my working theory about why you
lock up the house every time I drop by. It's either
that or you're afraid I'll sneak in and steal something."

I half-snorted. Then wished I'd laughed in a more
alluring and ladylike way.

He just smiled, though.

"But I figured it can't be the stealing because you
give me whatever produce I want."

"You come to fill up?" I gestured with my chin at
the bag in his hand.

"Maybe." He pulled at his ear and then looked me
straight in the eye in that playful calm way of his.

"Or maybe I'm just trying to figure you out, is all. Wondering if you'll ever let me in."

Now, this wasn't the fist-pounding on my door of all those boys who used to come around when I was younger. This was a question. And it wasn't about my kitchen, in case you didn't catch that. He wanted to know if I was open to things, and honestly, I didn't know. I mean, I did, but nothing is ever that simple. If the water witch weren't around, then I wouldn't have any trouble answering him.

"Can't," I said. "Where would I hide the bodies if I did?"

He laughed at the way I used his own joke against him and then gave me that look again. The one that made my insides melt and my head start spinning with thoughts I had no business having.

"What do you say we take a walk along the river-bank together one of these nights?"

"I can't," I blurted. I wanted to explain, but I didn't have the words.

He looked downright deflated at that and gazed long and hard at the closed door behind me, his voice whisper soft. "You think you're the only one with ghosts?"

I didn't have an answer for that, so I let the silence stifle us. He just ran his hands through his hair and headed on back to his land. He hadn't even bothered to fill up his bag. In fact, he'd left the Mercy Farm tote draped over my porch, as if he didn't have any need for it anymore.

He didn't play his records for me that night or for the rest of the week.

🝆

That silence filled up inside me until I thought my heart might break. I hadn't cried in some time, but I knew I'd done something wrong, and that was a new kind of pain. I couldn't stand the idea that I'd hurt a good man like Santos. I curled up in bed, held the mason jar to my lids, let that sorrow out until there was no more left in me, and put it in the spare room where I now stored all my tear-filled jars.

Then I thought long and hard about what to do next. It occurred to me that I didn't want to be like Sherry. When I look back at that night, I know it wasn't just La Llorona's fault about how things went down. I mean, yeah, she was terrible, and I still fantasized about holding her head under water until her limbs went soft and the muddy riverbank sucked her under. But Sherry had her part to play, too. She was so close to getting out, and she went and ruined it like she was more afraid of her own freedom than she was the woman at the bottom of the river. I didn't want to be afraid of life like that, afraid of letting good things in.

It scared me to admit it, but I deserved to enjoy the life I made for myself, without always thinking about that cold, wet scar along my shoulder or feeling guilty about how things went down with Sherry. And if I didn't start appreciating the life I'd built, well then, I was just as bad as La Llorona. Seemed to me she didn't want me happy, so if I kept myself from being happy, I mean, really truly happy, I was doing her a favor. I didn't like making things easy for her. I couldn't change the past. Not what happened to Sherry and not what happened to me. But I didn't have to stay there.

It was time I moved on with things.

So, the next day, I went about setting things right with Santos. I couldn't fix things right away because I had to be up early and go into the city to sell my wares at the Esperanza Growers' Market. I thought about him all the way into the city and all the way back. I wanted to know more about him—his passions, his plans for his land, even his ghosts. He was right to chastise me for acting like I was the only one fighting baptisms and demons. I wanted to hear his story and share mine with him, too.

I was cleaning out my market stall at the end of the day when I saw the biggest and brightest sunflowers wrapped with a fat blue ribbon in the booth across the way. Those sunflowers made me think of Santos and how he was big and tall and full of light, so I traded the last of my turnips for them and headed straight home. I didn't even bother unloading my truck when I got back to Mercy Farm, just went straight to Santos's porch and banged on his door.

He opened it but didn't come outside. He leaned against the doorframe and looked awfully handsome in a faded gray t-shirt and jeans and bare feet. Smelled good, too, like he'd just showered and used some of the fancy soap he was always making.

Now that I was in front of him, all the words dried up in my mouth, so I just held the sunflower bouquet tight and tried to get my bearings. He crossed his arms and waited.

"I don't like the river—no, that's not true." I took a deep breath and told him something I'd only ever talked about with Sherry. "I just can't be there after dark, and that's got nothing to do with you."

Some of the coldness left him, and he looked at me the way he used to. The way I liked him to.

Like I was Miracle Mercy. He raised his chin to the sunflowers.

"Those from your man?"

"These are for you." I shoved the bouquet into his hands. "I saw them at the market, and they made me think of you."

"Mercy." It was a sweet relief to hear my name across his lips again. I could see a soft blush creep along his dark skin. "Don't you know that's not how it's supposed to work?"

"What's that supposed to mean?"

"It means women don't bring men flowers."

I arched a brow and looked him dead in the eye. "Well, maybe they should."

I'd never seen that man speechless before, and it felt good to give him something to think about for a change.

♦

The music came back that night. The desert rose song to start and end the evening, and I slept better than I had all week, drought or no. I woke up with all sorts of thoughts, too. I thought maybe I'd bring over a bottle of wine sometime or invite him over here and do who knew what. It was a nice feeling to think there might be someone in this house besides me. I mean, once I let them in, those thoughts just kept coming.

I'd figure my way around this drought and what to do to keep the farm going. I wanted to visit Santos's farm, too—I'd stopped thinking of it as Mr. Consuelo's old farm by then—and get a proper tour. I wanted to hear about him and his ghosts. I was even eyeing a dress the color of the sunflowers I bought Santos in one of the shops in the city. I thought it might be nice to own a dress like that and wear it from time to time. I also thought—and this one will get you—that I might finally open up that old Seduction Red lipstick I'd kept in my vanity drawer all those years and try some on.

I might even consider dancing.

♦

It wasn't until the next morning that I realized I had gone a whole day without thinking about La Llorona, baptisms, or the bone-deep ache in my shoulder. In fact, when I reached back there, my shirt was nice and dry, not damp like it usually was.

It was a strange realization, considering I spent my youth afraid of her and more time than that thinking about her, hating her, and dreaming about baptizing her. I thought of the early days when I would fantasize about forcing her head into the water. I mean, I imagined drowning her down to every last detail: the way her hair clumped in my grip, the way she would thrash and fight me, and how good it would be to watch the life leach out of her until she went still. Then I'd let go and watch her body sink to the bottom of the river, never to be seen again.

When I wasn't fantasizing about baptizing her, I was thinking up ways to break her hold on me and if it would ever be possible to rescue Sherry. She terrorized my nights and haunted my days. I was frightened of her as a child, and that feeling only strengthened after that night on the river. Yet after seeing that one turnip burst to life with that one tear, and the utter silence that followed that evening, I made a marvelous discovery: La Llorona was afraid of me.

Good. She should be.

♦

I'm just about ready to wrap this whole story up, in case you were wondering, so stick with me.

The end came one day when Miguel was waiting on the porch as I headed out back. His head was hung low, and he had placed a bag on the porch, so I knew something was up. He held his hat in his hands and his dark hair was wild and unruly around his face, kind of like mine always was. He was too thin, and his features were too sharp to be called handsome, but he had this ethereal quality about him that kind of drew a person to him. That and his sincerity. He was just so himself.

I'd just come back from dropping off another basket at Sherry's back door. She was still covered in bruises, but lately, well, there was something different about her. Her hair seemed dryer somehow, her eyes less bloodshot. There was a darker blush to her cheeks, and I swear the last time I saw her in town, it was like she knew me.

She had been staring at the dollar cart that sat outside the bookstore, the one we used to comb for romance novels, and when she looked up and saw me, I think she really saw me. Didn't say anything, though. Just put the book she was looking at down and walked on down the street. I went and bought the book she held—*Love's Surrender*—and made sure to give her that book and extra turnips in her basket. Then I got a letter from Mr. Consuelo saying he'd met a pretty widow, and I could just hear the wedding bells that would come next, and I was happy for him. So, all by way of saying, I was feeling pretty darn hopeful that morning. But Miguel's worried face was enough to suck the joy right out of me.

"Miss Mercy," he said, his eyes wide and sorrowful and so darn earnest, I couldn't take it.

He was gonna say something bad, I knew it. And for a moment, all my hopes evaporated, and my heart got tight, and that cold chill gripped my shoulder. Why did I have to go and get so happy? I should have known it wouldn't last.

"I told you it's just Mercy."

"Mercy." I could see sweat beading his dark skin. "I'm afraid I haven't been completely honest with you."

Lord, I braced myself for the worst. "Go on then, tell me."

"My name's not really Miguel."

I stared at him, and his eyes were so big, I thought he might cry. I just laughed in relief and wondered if this was how Santos felt when I said strange things. "All right. So, what is it, then?"

"It's Jesse. Jesse James, Miss Mercy. Mercy." He clutched his hat like it was the only thing keeping him together.

I could see why he didn't like his name, but I didn't tell him so. His mom probably named him when she was drunk and never bothered to change it once she sobered up. She was cut from the same cloth as Sherry's mom, alternating between God and Jack Daniels.

"That's okay," I said. "I used to think I was more
of a Margarita or a Josephina before I grew into a
Mercy."

"But my name's terrible. I sound like a cheap
knockoff of some cowboy."

"Don't worry," I said. "You'll grow into it."

Then we both laughed at what I said, but I didn't
bother to correct things. Then we got to work.
Miguel-Jesse-James weeded while I went around
the property checking on things, and then together,
we harvested the week's produce. We worked later
than usual—all through the day—because Miguel
kept saying he'd just do this one last thing and then
another until the day was done, like he was stalling.

When we'd picked all we could that day, I sat back
on my heels and looked at Miguel-Jesse-James.
"There's something else, isn't there?"

Miguel—Jesse, I guess—looked at me with those
honest eyes and said, "Yeah. I'm leaving."

"When?"

"Soon. Tonight."

"That have anything to do with that man you've
been talking to? That Dr. Midnight?"

A few weeks ago, a stranger came to Sueño in a
beautiful canary yellow caravan that was so strange
and otherworldly, it could have only come from the
Shadow Lands. I'd seen him a time or two parked
by the river, but I never bothered with the man.

"Yeah," Miguel-Jesse-James admitted. "He's a
head doctor, and he's offered to train me up as his
apprentice."

I thought about all the new ideas Jesse had
been having lately. This sense that he knew more
and more who he was—not a Miguel but a Jesse
James—and I knew it was the right thing for him,

even if I didn't want anything to do with the Shadow Lands or traveling head doctors.

"Good for you," I said and meant it.

I figured if he was old enough to be his own man and leave, he was old enough to share a glass of wine. So, we had one to celebrate his leaving. We finished up around the farm and headed back to the porch.

"You tell Santos?" Miguel—Jesse—had been doing extra work for Santos, too, and I knew the older man would want to say goodbye.

Jesse said he wanted me to know first, but he was going to say goodbye to him on his way to Mr. Midnight's caravan. I eyed the satchel he'd brought as I popped back in the house for wine and glasses. So, he wasn't even going back home then.

"You make sure he gives you some of his salves, soap, anything you might need for the road." I knew Santos would insist on it, but Jesse was one of those people you had to make sure knew it was okay to take a kindness. I should know—I was one of them, too.

I poured us each a glass, and we settled on the porch to celebrate his leaving. It was one of those fine summer nights where the setting sun softened the heat, and everything felt vital and lazy at the same time. The mountains were a lush purple in the distance, despite the drought. We talked about books and took in the beautiful land before us.

"You ever think of leaving?" he asked as I poured more wine into his cup.

"Can't," I said. "So that means you'll have to have enough adventures for the both of us."

I usually ignored the bruises that showed up on his arms on a weekly basis because he'd made it clear he didn't want to talk about them, but tonight, I finally asked him, "Those boys give you those?"

I meant, of course, his momma's beaus and the kids around town his age that were bigger and meaner than him and liked to let the world know it.

He was quiet for so long, I didn't think he'd answer—then he did, and it just about broke my heart. "Sometimes."

He didn't have to say the rest. His mother was the *all the time* he couldn't voice. Then it occurred to me that it wasn't only men who did the hurting, which I felt right stupid about the second I thought it. Wasn't that La Llorona's way after all? A woman hurting people because she hurt too much to know better? And didn't I know a handful of men who wouldn't hurt a fly?

"I wish you would've told me," I said. "You could have stayed—"

"I know." He cut me off, and I thought I'd overstepped, then he shrugged and went on. "It was mine to deal with."

That I understood. There were some things in life that only you and you alone could handle.

Jesse ran his thumb up and down the lip of the small mason jar we used as glasses and bit his lower lip. "Just don't..."

"What?"

"You know...don't do to my momma what you did to your friend's momma." He buried his statement in a gulp of wine, and he refused to make eye contact with me.

I laughed at that. "You mean all this time you thought I was a witch and still came to work for me?"

He turned red and sheepish at that. "I mean, I always figured you were a nice witch. It's not like you cursed a good woman or anything."

We both laughed at that. I promised I wouldn't do anything to his momma, and I meant it. She wasn't my demon to deal with. Anyway, it was funny to think back at how scared I'd once been of Mr. Consuelo, thinking he was a murderer, but I'd no choice but to beg for work. I'm glad I did, and I'm glad Miguel came my way, too.

"It's not that she doesn't deserve it," he said. "It's just that I don't want to go and get you in trouble for something I have to handle. Town's finally forgetting about that last incident, and you deserve your peace."

I looked at him in the fading light. He probably wasn't around when I killed Sherry's mom, but old gossip dies hard, so it wasn't a surprise that he grew up hearing stories about the crazy witch that lived near the river. What did surprise me was that he worked up the courage to come work for me with those rumors still floating around.

He must've been desperate.

"Jesse?"

"Yeah?"

"You and I both know this town never forgets anything."

He laughed at that. "Sure wish it would. Least once in a while."

"Amen," I said in the closest thing I ever came to a proper prayer these days.

We finished our drinks in companionable silence, watching the sunset and enjoying the quiet symphony of crickets and cicadas before Santos started in with his records.

Then I did something I hadn't done since me and Sherry were friends, not even when Mr. Consuelo went away. I gave Jesse a hug. Then I paid him his wages with a little extra for his travels. He almost didn't take it, but I insisted, like the way Mr. Consuelo did when he gave me his tractor all those years ago.

"Go on now," I told him when it looked like he might tear up. "Make sure to send a postcard from time to time to tell me all about those adventures of yours."

I went to bed thinking about how I might share a glass of wine like that with Santos, and it was a mighty fine thing to see Jesse James taking the reins of his own life like that. That boy had so many good ideas floating around in that head of his. I just knew he would do interesting things with them. That luscious energy filled my chest, and the last thing I thought before falling asleep was that I couldn't remember being happier.

♦

I found Sherry's body washed up down river the next morning.

Her body was pale and bloated like a week-old fish, stringy black hair wrapped around her throat like a rope. But I knew it was her, even with the long drab dress with more buttons than style. Nothing like the real Sherry would have worn. But it was her body all the same, down to the thick scar on one palm that mirrored mine.

People would later call it a tragic accident or a strange disappearance. The word "suicide" might even have been whispered when her husband wasn't around. But I knew the truth.

This was La Llorona's doing. I should have known the idea of a kid like Miguel-Jesse-James leaving would make her fly into a rage. Should have known that Sherry holding that paperback would make her sick with hatred. Heaven forbid, I start thinking about sharing my nights with someone other than her. She couldn't bear to see us—any of us—moving on with our lives and leaving her behind just like her husband did.

I knew what she wanted me to do, too.

She wanted me to weep and moan and break. But I'd been weeping all my life and had no tears left. Seeing my friend's lifeless body—I wouldn't let it make me bitter. That was exactly what La Llorona wanted. Instead, I would make a home for Sherry in the earth, so the red clay would remind her of who she was before her baptism. I would dig a three-by-six womb for her, so she could return to who she could have been. When I laid her in the earth, I would release all my guilt and shame and fear with her. They would be the compost, the things that needed to die and disintegrate, to fertilize her body so that she would grow into something beautiful in the afterlife.

Sherry never understood my love of the land and its love for me. In the end, we would make sure that the last thing her body knew on this earth wasn't river water in her lungs or fists in flesh, but sunlight and dry land.

I couldn't leave her there. Now that I'd seen her, La Llorona might take her back into the river if I left to get a wheelbarrow to carry her home in. Or someone else might find her and tell her husband,

and he'd make sure she got a proper church burial. I didn't care what anybody thought, I wouldn't leave her trapped in a church coffin for all eternity. At least if she was put to rest on my land, like my mother was, she could choose her own path moving forward.

Her body would never be found. People would go through the motions of searching for her and putting up altars and praying for her soul—hell, they might even try knocking on my door asking about her if they could get past my ward—but after a while, they would forget her. Everybody loved a juicy tragedy, but nobody wanted to linger over anything that stank of La Llorona. They might not talk about her, might not ever acknowledge her, but they knew. They'd always known. They just swept it under the rug, like they did every bad thing in this town, and promised never to talk about it. So, things would eventually settle, and Sherry's God-fearing husband would go back to his drinking and, after a proper mourning period, would marry his mistress who was already heavy with his child, probably a son.

I flipped Sherry over so she was on her back and began dragging her home by her underarms. A little way into the Bosque, my arms gave out, and I fell back, hitting my ass hard on the dirt path. Sherry was so heavy with muddy river water that I wasn't sure I could carry her home on my own. But then a soft breeze ran its fingers through my hair and caressed my face, and I knew I wasn't alone.

I grabbed a fistful of Sherry's thick wet hair and started walking back to the farm. The breeze helped ease the weight of her body as the wild globe mallow scattered across our path softened things, like they always did, smoothing the road with soft dirt and leaves, while the Russian olive and cotton-wood roots pushed Sherry along behind me.

Eventually, I got her body back to Mercy Farm.

I'd wanted to show Sherry what I'd done with all those dreams of ours, but I'd always thought it'd be when she was better. Now I looked at her bloated, wet skin and glassy, bloodshot eyes at my feet. I hoped there was enough of her spirit left to take in what you could do if you just fought a little harder, if you just trusted enough in the possibility of having a two-story home and a place to put a bouquet of roses. But I knew it was no use.

What was done was done.

I left her just beside the porch while I went into the house for a bucket of warm water, some of Santos's lemon balm soap, a towel, a pair of scissors, and a brush to comb the river out of her hair. First thing I did was cut off that God-awful dress from her body and throw it in the trash. I took a minute just to process all the black and blue and yellow covering the skin under it. I mean, I knew all about this, of course, but it was different seeing it tattooed on all over her. I held her open palm in mine and traced her scar with my fingers, thinking about how fearless we once were.

Then I took my time washing her body, letting the sunny smell of lemon balm wash over us and soften my grief. I combed out her hair, so her thick, black curls could coil naturally around her head as they dried. Then I laid her out on a towel and let her dry in the sun, so she wouldn't go into the earth too pale.

In the end, Sherry let her sadness take her. There was nothing I could do about that. Not now, not that night on the river so long ago, not all those years I left baskets by her back door. It had been foolish of me to try to save her. I should have never put that on myself. I knew that now. I knew it the same way I knew I had to keep moving forward or drown in the sorrows of the past.

Here's the thing about miracles—medicine—whatever you want to call it. You can't force it on anyone or do the work for them. All you can do is make your own miracles and let people live out their lives however they plan to. And I don't much care if you think that's over-explaining things. This is my story, and I'll tell it the way I want to. You don't have to keep listening if you don't like what I have to say. Just know that some things are worth saying outright.

I'll say this outright, too, since I'm on a roll here: I will have a good man in my life, just like Sherry's aunt. There's nothing the town or La Llorona can do to stop that from happening. And when I find this man, his fists will go into the soil, not faces, planting herbs and love and life, not bruises or ugly feelings. He will know how to use the sun and fertile soil to grow things. And he will know that our daughters should never roam the riverbeds alone. Him and me, we'll tell our girls outright about how things are, so that river witch can't feed on the shadows and the silence. We'll teach them how to hone their affinity for the land, too, so they don't have to struggle to figure things out on their own like I did. I've thought of this for so long and so hard that I know it to be true. What's more, I think this man will be really good at making lemon balm soap.

Anyway, while Sherry dried, I went to the back of my lot where there was some stubborn soil that wouldn't grow anything I planted there. It just kept telling me that it wasn't the spot for the things I wanted to grow there, so I finally gave up and figured it'd tell me what it wanted there in its own time. The land was like that. It gave a lot, but it expected a lot, too. Mostly that you didn't force anything on it that it didn't want, and I understood that.

Today, though, I just knew that I had the perfect seeds for this empty patch of earth and dug a hole in the ground as deep as I could. I wanted the earth to hold Sherry, remind her that she was red clay and warm brown soil. I wanted her to know, in the end, how good life could be if you let it.

I could feel Santos watching me from his side of the coyote fence, and I thought maybe it was time to explain things to him. Why my shoulder always hurt a little, and why I couldn't ever take bubble baths. Why I had a thick scar across one palm. Why Sherry's dead body lay drying in the sun. I was tired of carrying around this burden alone.

But first, I had some things to take care of.

Once I'd dug the hole, I went back to the house and filled my wheelbarrow up with as many mason jars as I could and hauled them out to my plant rows. It took me most of the day, but I managed to empty each and every one across my rows of crops, all the while thinking of vital growing things and lemon balm soap and that one song about the wild desert rose. When I'd finally emptied out my spare room of every last mason jar, I hauled the last of them out to that back corner where I'd dug that hole.

Then I went back to the house for one more thing. Remember that fat bouquet of red, red roses Santos had given me? I'd been keeping the seeds from that close by for some time. I kept those flowers alive as long as I could, in my bedroom, because I liked them close at night, not the entryway like I thought I would all those years ago. Once their buds had begun to fade, I asked them to give up their seeds so I could hold on to that special gift. They listened, the way my turnip seeds listened, and the way my squash and beans listened when I told them they needed to reach up along the trellises I made for them.

That bouquet had withered and dried and formed its flowers into rosehips that spilled their seeds for me. I collected them in a tiny jar and had kept them on my vanity table ever since. Now it was time to put them into the ground. I slipped them into one of my overalls and went out to get Sherry.

I grabbed the towel she was on and used it to drag her to her new home. She was dry now, her hair a riot of curls around her. I liked to think her skin looked a little warmer, the bruises less ugly, though that was probably just my wishful thinking. In any case, she was free to move on from all of that.

I gave her hand one last squeeze and kissed her forehead. I thought of saying something, but in the end, I didn't have words any more than I had tears to give. So, I lay Sherry into the ground as gently as I could and, with her, buried this whole sorrowful story.

I sprinkled those rose seeds over her body and pushed the dirt over her, all the time thinking I was done being La Llorona's unfinished business. Done making everything about her. Slowly, methodically, I used the last of my mason jar tears to water Sherry's grave as I thought about moving on. I thought of beeswax candles and old records and the best turnips you'll ever eat. I thought of sunflower yellow dresses and smutty paperbacks. I thought that Sherry deserved to have as many roses as she wanted. I thought of so much and not one of those thoughts had anything to do with La Llorona.

She was the Weeping Woman, sure. But I was the woman who made rainwater out of tears. I would use them to water my crops through this drought. When people bought my fat turnips and sharp radishes and long, thick carrots, they would taste of freshly turned earth and freshly turned futures, hope, the bittersweet taste of things past, and the salty tang of possibility. This I would do to remind others that we are the seeds we plant, not the histories forced upon us. This I would do to wash away the sorrow from my soul.

Was I still scared? You bet.

But nothing makes a woman brave except living.

I got to thinking that maybe I did want to dance. But not with just anyone, mind you. I let my eyes stray to the lush farmland next door. I took in my adobe home, Mercy Farm, the hollyhocks along the fence, the rows of produce freshly watered with all those stockpiled tears, and the mound of empty mason jars on my patio. I mean, I really saw this whole life I built for myself. All this started with thoughts. The house. The farm. The man waiting for me on the other side of that fence. Really, really good thoughts.

When I'd emptied the last of those mason jars, I sat back on my heels. Waited. And watched as seeds began to crack open, sprout, and push through the grave dirt one green tendril at a time.

Finally, all those tears put to good use.

ABOUT THE AUTHOR

D r. Maria DeBlassie is a native New Mexican mestiza and award-winning writer and educator living in the Land of Enchantment. She writes about everyday magic, ordinary gothic, and all things witchy. When she is not practicing her brujeria, she's teaching classes about bodice rippers, modern mystics, and things that go bump in the night. She is forever looking for magic in her life and somehow always finding more than she thought was there. Find out more about Maria and conjuring everyday magic at www.mariadeblassie.com.

Follow Maria DeBlassie

FACEBOOK
| TWITTER
| YOUTUBE |
I
NSTAGRAM

ALSO BY THE AUTHOR

Fiction
Hungry Business: A Gothic Story about the Horrors
of Dating

Non-Fiction
Practically Pagan: An Alternative Guide to Magical
Living
Everyday Enchantments: Musings on Ordinary
Magic & Daily Conjurings